Obscui

Obscure Reflections at Dawn

eBook ISBN: 979-8-88757-423-3
Paperback ISBN: 979-8-88757-424-0
Hardback ISBN: 979-8-88796-833-9

Contact: jackclubbauthor@gmail.com

Contents

For my mother

Obscure Reflections at Dawn

JACK CLUBB

Ha-Aretz

Part One
Ritual to Rid Thyself of an Enemy

"The atoms must be used over and over again; thus,
the death of one thing becomes necessary
for the birth of another."
-Lucretius

Chapter I
A rebirth through tragedy

1

There was darkness...

Slowly, the shadows recede as the red stage curtains are raised aloft and a scene of gloom fades into view. Like a slide show from an old projection reel that suddenly bubbles from the heat, then warps the film, skipping upon the loop.

Click! Click! Click!

A light flickers, reflecting off the stone walls. The room smelled like Spikenard and incense. All at once I felt as if I was hit in the head with a hammer.

Thud! Thud! Thud!

Doubling over in pain, I swung my arms around to ward off the attack.

After a few moments, my energy being exhausted, I collapsed.

I was alone. *Had*, been alone.

With the pounding of my heart and an accompanying flashing light the image collapsed, therefore withdrew, and finally exploded into my consciousness.

A Grandfather Clock was ticking backward from somewhere yet previously unknown to me. Vividly, through my mind's eye, I beheld a vortex of souls being dragged around the *Cosm* by its inertial wake that it was creating for itself.

It was the eternal *Nechash*. The great behemoth. Bound and wrapped amid the *Tohu Vavohu* on its course of chaos and *Ohr*.

The scene unfolding was that of a great clockwork of parts, biomechanical in nature. It pummeled through the endless expansion of its own inoculated existence. As if the cogs were in slow motion because I was simply observing it through the hourglass of time.

Click, click. Thud! Click, click. Thud!

The tempest just dragged the bodies in and thereupon, spat them back out on its violent path. It was the serpent that consumes itself, making a macabre broken figure eight in its course of perpetual motion that was being lit with the fusion of creation.

In flashes. A memory, or a dream…

Tick. Tock. Tick. Tock! Tick. Tock.

Reality, taking a good enough hold and not letting go this time, relinquished me unto the present.

Setting up, and taking in my surroundings with a vividness of sight, I felt my head. It hurt so bad that I started to reel again. I simply needed to relax, then the pain would soon ease, I was sure.

Several moments later, collecting myself, I checked for injury. I found no blood. Well, at least that was good. Gazing around, I tried to remember the last time I had fallen asleep or lost consciousness.

Nothing…

It would be fine, I knew. I just needed to not panic and try to think clearly. Taking a deep breath, I closed my eyes once again.

A moment later, upon opening them and gazing about, I found myself in a vast room or crypt of some kind. It appeared like a movie set or like that of a dungeon. Only this place was modern *Ish,* in way of electricity and everyday appliances. The remains of a fire that was going in the hearth was burning down to its last grain of ashes.

Many objects filled the subterranean dwelling. Most notably, a suit of armor with a strange cross tattooed into the front of it, deep down into the steel. A four-poster bed occupied the corner. A giant wooden desk was in the center and it looked like a wardrobe on the far eastern end. Here was a chair with lions' feet, the kind from the Vermeer paintings. In the chair was a mannequin, or was it, a man?

It *was* a man. He was sitting upright, as if asleep, in quiet contemplation.

'Tread lightly,' my inner voice whispered, *'Do not disturb him. For he looks to have a dark ambivalence about himself.'*

Slowly, I began to make my way around the macabre chamber.

See? Look there, an Egyptian sarcophagus…

-And here, an ancient abacus, counting the arcs of doom upon thy peg of years. Strange vapors, appearing like that of fog, followed my steps, sending small phantoms into rapture along my path, just to be snuffed out again and then spent right back up into the ether.

If one listened close enough sounds could be heard like that of a far-off hum. Perhaps a furnace or generator, purring to the quickening breath of despair.

Approaching the old hermit, he looked as if to be sleeping. However, on closer inspection, he was clearly dead. Something told me to put my head down in reverence. Nevertheless, the room took on a darker gloom than before.

The crackling of the fire had ceased and I perceived that somehow the shadows in the domicile had grown darker and somehow lengthier. Which was strange, for there were no windows visible. The light source was thence provided by four big lamps that were set deep within the recessed bowers. The ceiling, having a bit of vault to it, was frescoed and adorned with scenes from '*The Lamentation of the Magi.*'

An unseen force, like that of a magnet, drew my eyes to a piece of art that hung on the wall, in a guild frame. It had a handwritten note along with a page that was neatly cut from a book and ornately constructed so that it was bound perfectly within the glass.

Looking a bit closer, it read:

"The occupants of the room seemed to stare in solitary ineptitude. All were lost amid the realm of lucid dreams. Appearing like twisted marionettes or broken mannequins, delivered unto the Grand Theater of Gal. Their forlorn eyes, took on a blank and pale quality, illuminating them from within. Now, when they beheld, they would behold with purpose. To consume the loss and give birth to a new dawn. A rebirth through tragedy."

- 'Patriarchs of the Eternal Flame.'

Then below that, in red ink:

"-to Edward, I wish you nothing but the best."

Strange passage. There was no signature.

Wondering as to its origins, I began to feel light-headed but not wanting to disturb anything that currently occupied the chamber, I sat down cross-legged on the floor. As I did so, I noticed there was a curious star engraved into the stone bedrock. Closing my eyes to meditate and ask the elements for guidance, I tried to put together the events of how I got here. The first and last thing I could remember was taking in the current abode with my head thumping. Feeling like my brain would pop right out of my skull.

This must have produced a very bizarre scene. Me meditating on the floor, a corpse reclining in a chair in the corner, like all was completely normal.

Deciding to get back up and search for answers, the most pressing question being, where was the exit? The only practical way to get an answer was to follow the walls, I presumed. Deeply studying them for a moment, they seemed to recede, appearing as if there were crawling things in the shadows, I shuttered.

The dead body held the answers. Maybe I should ask him?

Searching my bag's contents, I found the proper incense and symbols needed to rouse the old man, for I have just a humble amount of arcane knowledge to try and take this operation a bit further.

After making my cleansing invocations and opening proxy, I put my left hand on the shoulder of the dead man as I held up my right to receive the *thaumaturgy*.

Standing amid this ready-made magus circle, I began to feel the change taking place. A light tempest sprang to manifest and the smell of burning sulfur permeated the aperture within.

All at once, it was as if I was struck by lightning. This person had a miraculous amount of stored energy; however weak, it beat with a soft pulse. This is an indication that this soul was trapped in perdition, between that bridge of divergence.

At this point, I had to break the connection, for it was too strong. I could tell this reaction had sparked an awakening of sorts, so I tried to re-establish a momentary fusion within the corpse.

Suddenly, I could hear distant popping sounds, and combusting Tesla Coils, amid small strings of existing reality, that was producing the room's fog. Then, that same dense fog started to reverse into an unseen vacuum. At first, it appeared innocent enough. However, as it consumed the vapors that were about, it subsequently first pulled in my hand, then, my entire being within itself. The last thing I remember thinking was that I would never fit through that small opening.

I lost consciousness, and fell into a cold slumber…

2

Fade in: The scene was of a Neoclassical nature. There was the aroma of wine and bittersweet sulfur that was so much more sufferable after crossing over that event horizon. That midpoint of the dream world, and this, realized one.

At once, the sounds of a party close by reminded me of Bacchus and all of his friends together. From the sweet laughter of the girls' voices, I was curious as to the nature of the assembly. When they audibly receded, I was left with the song of birds, which began to make a far-off den, signaling their departure.

Presently, just out of frame, I heard the heavy trample of many footsteps and beheld the most fantastic supernatural event that I had thenceforth witnessed. It was the physical manifestations of the Oreads. A long processional knot of unnaturally twisted nymphs. Each one, in turn, soared up into a *maelstrom*. Just to fall back down in unison, like on a modern-day children's slide. Then, landing to run and be caught right back up again, swept into the furor of the tempest. Some were laughing, some were not.

Over my head, then down into the crystal waters of the stream at my feet. There looked to be no less than five scores in all. In the distance, they came running, as if lightning had struck them, sending them into preternatural ecstasy. All their nude bodies, being covered only here and there with bits of fabric, albeit coiling like they were all a part of a choreographed ballet, being bent unto the centrifuge. It was a bit discerning, amidst this strangling breeze, for I had failed to notice that they were all part of an eternal hunt of some kind, being driven forth by some unseen beast.

I wondered as to who this was that pursued the creatures so vehemently? Then, listening closely for a moment, I soon realized it was none other than *Diana*, that queen of the hunt, who provided the chase, and I, standing witness to this spiraling *omniform*.

The pursuer, was faster than any of these other creatures, for I could see her as lightning leaves a trail, or as a volcano spits forth its burning lava.

As predicted, past she came, bounding over a stump that was eight feet tall or more. Springing upon a fallen elm, she bounded even higher than that, exceeding twenty feet into the air. A moment later, and she was gone.

I was left with just a sixteenth of a second to regard her totality. However, I saw that she had a crescent-shaped moon that was projected from her crown. I subjectively contemplated the sacred feminine and quieted a storm, for I was quickly joined in my present vicinity by three goat/men, well, Satyrs. They, being of the likes of Silenus or Pan, after their kind.

Sure enough, a few moments later, two more Satyrs ignorantly ran past, not even noticing I was there. Though, nevertheless, I knew I was of physical existence because I had a short length of a shadow.

The women were flying and slipping forth vehemently, albeit, in witnessing that only these devil men have such eyes of lust. Though, astonished as they were and the way they looked upon the women, I wondered how it would all play out.

A bit of water splashed as they went by. I had never seen anything as supernatural as this. At once, out to my left-hand side, beyond the stand of trees, there resided a truly remarkable specimen to gaze upon. It was an angel, or angelic being, or at least resembling such.

She was startling to behold.

Fallen like man, were my enchantments for being obsessed by this creature. The only way I can describe it is, inoculated wonder. Being so encapsulated by her charms, I could tell that this was a true representation of the celestial court. Her figure and beauty quickened a new furor within. Furthermore, I was always under the singular impression that angels didn't have a gender, so to speak.

Then, watching her disappear behind the clearing into the Elms, I followed in that direction. All the while, I was aware of the feelings she had so passionately incited from within, producing such forms that were previously unknown. Though, not exactly yearning or lust, something else, just beneath the surface.

As I rounded the corner at the saplings and realized she had such continence on her face that she appeared to be solemn, though wise. Reminding me of the porcelain drama masks, that are sleek and clean in their perfection yet, bound to break.

It was evening here, though at first it was hard to tell, for the shadows were in the wrong spots and not at all what I was used to. The Angel was about forty feet away in a small grove that was tucked away, sitting resigned on her knees and her head was slightly bowed as if she were in deep contemplation.

Descending to the courtyard, I noticed her sitting upon the grass, adorned with roses of adoration. On her back were two big magnificent wings. They appeared as those in the form of an Eagle. They were extended just off the ground. Fluttering, as would blink an eye, or beating, as would a heart.

There was a rock of memorial before her and I thought it must be from some former acquaintance whom she mourned.

Reaching the lower ground, I felt the ever-so-pressure and then release, of some unknown magnetic force that had granted me access to this sacred area. When I had gotten closer, I coughed lightly so as to not surprise the supernatural Shekinah.

She turned with an amused look on her alien face. Gazing toward the rock, she began to speak and said: *"Does thou presume to enter this place of solitude and mourning?"* she asked without looking into my eyes, choosing to look off into the distance instead. She seemed so extraordinary in her malevolence. "*Day imparts the eve gloom, thou fast bends to lick the wounds, so deep*," she sang.

It seemed as if a light veil had sunk over the western horizon, producing burnt oranges in hue upon the landscape. The colors worked marvels on the angelic creature's singular glyph of persona. Though, her gait held more enchantments than I can thus provide an adequate summary.

Presently. I longed for home. I wanted to get away from whence whatever dark magic had brought me here.

Looking a bit further into the distance, she began her tragic litany once again. Her voice was very unearthly, in that it was as if she had an entire choir following her dark lead, in concert with each other. I began to have visions flash in and out of my mind. These revelations were planting seeds to incubate, in turn, giving false promises that would pick at the blossoms of despair.

Then realizing the current situation again, I tried to collect myself.

The Angel was revealing these visions to me. When they came, they did so in violent flashes; in turn, I felt nauseous. My attention was soon stolen away by her enchanting voice.

"*The phoenix had been without life for many weeks, why?*" The questioning angel sang.

In answer, and not completely understanding, I asked, "from whence has thou brought thee from which I am alive, and an enchanter of small things?"

At once, my mind was gorged to the brim with scenes, though I only saw bits and pieces. Seeing how I had to have the information broken into smaller increments. The Angel, realizing that the visions were too much for me to handle, for she seemed to forget herself momentarily of the fact that I was mortal, and these circumstances had the power to alter one's fusion.

She was a magnificent being, at least seven feet tall. Not at all unlike those goddesses of myth.

As she unfolded her massive wings and flexed them, I noticed there was a fire about her eyes that was strange to behold, though this display was something I just could not altogether grasp, for I had never seen such fantastic creatures, and I suddenly became frightened.

She was looking down, a gothic statue, just her eyes and mouth, barely perceptibly moving. "*Who art thou? What have thou come for thence?*"

Stammering, I said, "I am just a humble Artist. My importance is not of value or care to anyone, except for those who thirst or crave for art."

In form of a reply, she turned and did a circuit about the grave. I say grave, for as she made the circumference; she carefully did not step on the area that would mark the spot that was the size of a man. Then, looking down with slight amusement on her face that was altogether different than that of a human's, seeming almost amphibious in nature, I became conscious of the fact that she was plainly reminding herself to do so. To be more human-like. Possibly, this was just her nature.

A curious circumstance fell upon me presently. As these visions started to appear as a form of communicating her ideas, she sent them in vivid flashes. Illuminating my third eye, like burning nails hammered into my forehead, one after another. That mystical *Ohr*, raining down in a rapturous deluge of information, arriving from splendid epiphanies.

Her kind was known as *Archons* or *Archonians*. They, being the opposite of their counterparts from *Quloph*, those that's blood runs cold, that of the *Naga*. Known collectively as *Demonbrood*.

Archonians, however, came from a set of *Celestial Spheres* of all their own, but with all things, its dual manifestation sported a dark stained reflection. Thus, revealing its violent nature as something that on this fantastic level has to be seen to be believed.

The *Archon*, revealing mountains and planets and long-hidden planes of existence known as The *Dementia*. This knowledge wasn't given freely, it came at a price. Some prices are more inflated than others, depending on relative positions therein, this also being the nature of things.

Redirecting my attention to her kneeling in front of the grave, her movements seemed broken. However, everything else seemed to be of a stop motion nature, and she, an unbound marionette set free to discover.

She, the fowl, and the fauna. All of it. All would stop, as if glitching at intervals, thereupon reanimating into the next frame. I knew I had to be missing something, voices carried on normal, albeit in strange high song at times. Why?

The sky turned an orangish purple in hue. I could hear the sounds ever so slightly switch from being dominated by birdsong, into the steady drone of crickets and locusts as if singing it all into existence.

The angel began once again: "*My fallen king upon this memorial I pride, who would have dreamed of an angel alive, carrying a longing inside. Cursed with this feeling unchanging, though feelings are not worth much to the destiny of an Archonian born,*" she sang solemnly, with arms outstretched. Though, I only caught a glimpse of her eyes as they closed upon her finishing the end of the verse.

Every time I looked at her, she was standing still, though in a different pose upon each separate observation. Cleverly moving each time, I looked away.

Strange.

I responded, "Weep no tears for the fallen, cursed with unmatched beauty, is you. A virtue in thorns and crowns. Angelic form, since when has thou cast solace in this place?"

At this foolish question, she looked off out into the distance. "*Not so long ago.*"

In my mind's eye and my reality, the scene changed. I was pulled amid that strange loop of a vortex, trapped amid a furor of souls. There were many correlating and parallel roads too and I was sure I would be consumed. For one microsecond, my hair started to be lifted and goosebumps pocked my skin. In slow motion, a big thick lightning bolt seemed to appear out of the ether and at once, hit me right in the face. As soon as I was struck, all I saw was white. A moment later, and I heard a loud crash as electricity began to weave a hum of its own accord, clashing realities together.

I was thrown this way and that. As I was born upon that bolt of lightning and was thrown out of the perpetual knot. The other coiling souls, plopping and thudding onto the ground, slowly levitated back up, up, and over.

Boom! Flop! Boom. Flop. An all repeating, never-ending, knot of infinity coiled on.

In all of The Heliosphere or the volcanic mountains in the land of hidden origins that was being revealed, there are said to be woods and mountains. In the *Ignatian Tower of Fears,* therein dwells that lurking bitch, *The Chaos Witch*, *Barrel Von Strain*, whose names are not meant to ever again be uttered upon the world of man.

My mind was confused about words and places that I did not know. Riding the lightning down onto a floor of atmospheric pressure, amid a rapture that beat upon this furtive land that has been *seen*. However now, could not be *unseen*. Mostly, men are not permitted such visions, for the men of this realm's minds are full of chaos and corresponding illusions that usually result in futility. All the miseries of life and its eternal sufferings, which is a condition of material existence, the vision thus revealed.

Realizing I was bound within the embrace of a *Merkabah*, that yielded its *Sphere of Existence* amid this *maelstrom*, I was somehow penetrating the astral and ether alike. A slimy black gel was the outer layer of the vehicle that was granting me passage. It was encased in the shape of a brain. An orange liquid being excreted ever and anon to be used as fuel. It seemed that nothing could penetrate the hub one bit.

There were mountains and people. Great animals and huge trains, bigger than the most prodigious I had ever seen.

Vast steel mills and bridges were built within gothic cathedrals. Protesters and police were amid the gangs and hollows, ghettos, and courtyards. Virgins and whores alike made clandestine deals with pimps.

Gods and Devils, as always, finding succor in human prayers and offerings, competed for the souls of the Inhabitants. This is the core of their immortality though, nevertheless, time has a way of outgrowing the old gods we create for ourselves. To gain control factions of strange militia and priests were everywhere it seemed, strove to dominate all that lurked within their shadows. Sowing the seeds of hate. However, these holy men and unholy men were not of the normal lot. This place is called, -I looked to her, for I did not know.

"Andalusia," she said, in that monotone voice that was distinct unto her.

"Andalusia," hearing it come off my tongue was interesting in the fact that there was a longing within the mere dictation of the word. It was to inspire dream vistas and haunted mountainous regions still unexplored by our clever race.

Suddenly it stopped. I was on solid ground once again. As I was made manifest amid a small furor of winds that were spent up, and around atoms cracked and popped and from these smoke vapors appeared forming faces that were trying to invade my Sphere of Existence. Distorted screams accompanied the visions that licked at the borders of my peripheral. Appearing as a translucent fog, the phantoms came and then began to be snuffed out, one by one. Only being held in check by a hand unseen.

Quickly, the smoke vapors evaporated into a distant pocket of memory, that I was somehow made to manifest within a fury of ashes. The electrons that lightly danced along the edges of this physical reality coalesced with scintillating *Ohr*. Then, suddenly, I felt myself being placed on solid ground.

I had arrived. Wherever *here*, was?

As the fog began to clear, I realized the angel had sent me hence from the courtyard of the garden, revealing to me who the rock of memorial was in dedication.

The first thing I noticed, was that it was stifling hot. Even in the gloom that I currently found myself in, all being a part of a vast room that was draped by heavy shadows. Hearing something slither in the dark, I quickly jumped so as to avoid the rat's companion that I had landed upon. Seeing a window amidst the flurry of dust particles I had sent scrambling in the heat of the room upon arrival, I saw the way outside. The way out only being barred by a couple of thin pieces of wood nailed to the window.

Swiftly, going in the direction of the light, as I was running from the rodent and halfway there to the window, when coming nearer to my senses, I collected my courage and honorably walked the rest of the way.

The rat steadily followed a pace behind. It was lucky that I didn't just liberate it unto the afterlife without delay, right then and there. Had I been so inclined, given its dejected state, it would have most likely welcomed such an end to this inoculation, considering it a favor. Maybe, it was going mad because it wasn't the one given unto eternity first, being only seconded by its former comrade or brother.

I played with the idea that it was speaking, *'Stop, it was saying. Stop!'* It was professing its resignation and unfair treatment in life. Valiantly throwing it all away, in the name, of death. To protest in the darkness of oblivion, before *The Court of Fools.*

At that point, silently saying goodbye to the rat forever, I shook my head like a drunk trying to get the world from spinning around. For them, being a side effect of the alcohol and inertia from the motion of the planet, though mine, was somehow an after effect of the quickening from the *Void* from which I had just thenceforth came.

Approaching the exit, I quickly started to remove the boards. Each one squeaking, setting my nerves to tremble, not knowing what I was in store for on the other side of the threshold. Thereupon carefully crawling out of the window, I stepped into another time, and into a world it seemed, that was not my own.

Taking in my surroundings, albeit being startled once again, I narrowly escaped complete collision with a veiled woman. She had on a drama mask and was covered in rags, baring her teeth, she hissed at me. When I showed her my fist, she just gave me a wicked look and paced off. I inadvertently followed her shadowy path in between a large cart and two stucco buildings. All at once, I realized the cart was just sitting in front of a much bigger edifice that occupied the square.

I was on the opposite side of an ominous castle. Presently, fully turning the corner, I was greeted by a fury of voices. Many townspeople were in attendance, monk, and maiden alike, dotting the vast cobbled street. However, one could tell that the assembly was here for the return of the *King* and his soldiers.

They all had on-white tunics over suits made of armor. There was a curious phenomenon about me as well, for they all too sported a drama mask, as did the woman I first encountered in rags. Of the strange faces the community wore, there were scarcely two that were alike. It seemed today was a masquerade or some such holiday though, what's more, is not every person assembled was sporting the disguise. My attention was stolen away as shouts of approval and cheers as The King and his retinue appeared around the bend causing all to go wild in a joined tirade of cheer and hollers.

There were many people in front of the castle to greet him and his attendants as he dismounted. Presently, a squire ran up to take the King's reigns. A couple of other *Knights* were clapping him on his shoulder as he passed. All were wearing the same white tunic with the same red cross on it. Every one of these men had masks of armor, some even had intricate scroll or leaf work ornamentation adorning the mirrored surface.

Now, all eyes fell upon the arrived King. After a few words from the soldiers, he moved his gaze to her.

The maiden.

At this, there were more shouts and applause as if on cue. The object of the King's attention, who was veiled in the season's latest fashions of mourning having most of her entourage adorned with matching face wear of archetypal variation and porcelain in appearance, just stood in the full rapture of his gaze. A Melancholy Madonna.

These, and other variables, all added to the macabre element of the dizzying factions, amid whose company I currently found myself.

She, the mournful maiden herself, being accompanied by other ladies and countesses of an alike nature, were all not dissimilar in dress to each other or in appearance. In the front row of the pavilion was the first to receive the royal line.

The King was presently lifting back his maidens veil, revealing a transcendent radiance. Feeling like I should not stare at this reunion, I searched my surroundings. Peering behind, there was a glass window. As I gazed into my reflection, I was startled to see that my eyes took on an illuminated quality of all their own. It must have been from looking upon the Angel. Seeing a bit different, everything was illuminated to me with a much greater sense of density.

Several caravans of townspeople were arriving. A moment later and there were more than two scores of the *Kings Knights* that had appeared and were beginning to dismount. Most were making similar greetings, with not so similar maidens.

Presently, out of the corner of my eye, I was surprised to see the angel standing amidst the people on a marble dais, completely still, like a mannequin. Only I seemed to notice that her eyes were moving, scanning the crowd. I was glad to see that no others had the curiosity to behold her authenticity.

This place was quite the medieval scene, feeling so frozen in time that I longed to haunt my own.

The Angel looked to be judging all from above, only now, mentally, for when I blinked, she had closed her eyes—playing the melancholy sentinel once again.

Suddenly, looking down, she exuded that strange light out of her half-closed eyes, still plainly visible, even on this bright summer day.

"*Hey*!" I yelled. Trying to get her attention, I saw she had gotten down off the dais and was slowly dropping back into the crowd.

At that moment, a short round man, who looked to be a butcher of sorts, dried blood all over his oversized apron, giant veins on meaty forearms, took notice of her.

Before long, it had to have been chance, for we both acted at the same time. "*What the fuck?*" He questioned when he was blinded by the glow from the unusual light her eyes gave off. The only problem was, that illusions were made for the dark; they don't belong to the day. The man had the momentary terror that I had experienced upon witnessing her charms. This was all just a fundamental part of her celestial nature, I had assumed.

I ran past him. As I did, he tried to grab my shirt. He had the strength of two men. Skillfully dodging his assault, I went in pursuit of the *Archonian*. It was so bright out that the metal of the different textures of armor was blinding, almost causing me to lose my footing at times. Finally, reaching the front of the pavilion set up to receive the *King and Queen,* the butcher was just behind me, when I looked off to my left in a small alcove, knelt like a monument to the fallen, was the angel, playing a statue.

Appearing as if from nowhere, the butcher was directly in front of me, made manifest.

"*I've been looking for you,*" he said as I put my hands on his shoulders in a reaction to try and thwart his advance. However, the scene changed yet again. A thick blanket of fog enveloped me and everything from the crowd and the angel disappeared among the mist. Swirling amidst the vortex of time everything slowed as it had before. As one in a lucid dream, I was jolted this way and that. In a flash of lightning, my physical nature was enchanted, seeming to chew me up and then spit me back out again.

I manifested upon a battlefield that was drenched in blood, damn near soaking the entire ground. It reminded me of one of hamlet's chosen haunts, except that this one had no epic dialogue or fancy swordplay; no, this one gave birth to only two children, *Murder and Killing.*

I had never physically seen a scale of violence this severe. Suddenly, I became afraid. My hands started to shake from nerves.

Then, a warm comfort fell over me, like a blanket of dark embraces.

"*Do not fear Artist; you are quite safe,*" the Archonian Angel said from several feet away. The smoke that surrounded her was dense.

Unaware until now, of the mingled sadness and guilt that this place bestowed upon its champions, I realized that something was so very wrong here. I mean, here I was, in the presence of a *holy Angel,* yet all the hatred around me was suffocating beyond measure, yet persisted, even in my celestial company.

I could descry wood and something else mingled with it. There were no masks of partygoers or lighthearted dalliances here. In this plot of earth, death and dying held sway.

"How many men fell this day?"

"More than a couple."

I was completely and utterly repulsed, and I was no more afraid. I was filled with pity and then anger. As I was contemplating this idea, it was as if *Zeus* had thrown one of his lightning bolts of fire at me once again, licking at my body as the electricity ran through all my bones and flesh. The atoms within and without, disengaged, unwrapping and I was gone again—through that *vortex.* It pulled me in to another place and time.

I was pushed this way and that, gaining another glimpse of that place, that land beyond *Ha-Aretz*, from which I was familiar.

Then, as quickly as I had been taken by the storm, I was shat out the other side of the *void.* The scintillating light illuminated the chamber in which I was made manifest. All of a sudden, with a flash, I was wrapped in a blanket of darkness once again. Closing my eyes to have them adjust to the gloom faster.

There were blinds on the windows, through which tiny slivers of light on the other side crept through the cracks. The lightning had caught a dried-up rose on fire. I snuffed it with the tips of my fingers. When it didn't go out at once, I bit back the urge to hiss. However, the only sounds were barely perceptible instruments being played, just beneath the silence.

I was in an antechamber of the Italian type. Hearing laughter from one of the adjacent rooms I approached a heavy oriental carpet that was draped over the threshold. A crack in the fold on one side was letting light in.

Peering through, I was surprised to see two maidens on their hands and knees, supporting a large dress. Then, noticing the woman with the warmest smile in the room she anxiously squealed at the others to hurry. Her pear-shaped breasts and nipples were in the shape of rose petals, bouncing a bit.

There was a disturbance out in the hall, sounding like an entire company or retinue of men. The girls whispered that it was the *'King and his entourage.'* Immediately, I realized this woman was his soon-to-be *Queen.* If not that, then *whore.*

She let out a short cry. Hissing at both maidens she said, "*Hurry, he is to presently arrive.*"

One of the women reminded her this was just the fitting. "Princess, you won't be wed for two more weeks!"

"*Still, though,*" the Princess replied softly. "*I don't want him seeing me adorned as such, Scarlet.*" She said, addressing the first. "*Take my mask, and hand me the other,*" the woman diligently complied.

They quickly lowered the royal wedding dress and she stepped to the side into a less regal outfit, though still holding the same semblance of accord as the other.

Next, they adjusted her evening gown and quickly started to pull it up. Just as they finished doing so, the King came in. "*My love*," he proclaimed. At once, rushing to her, she gave him that resplendent smile once again.

From the open window a shadow was lengthening just past the panes, and to my surprise, it was the *Archonian*. She landed without a sound. Then, malevolently levitated just without the window seal. Quietly surveying the room, she began looking fondly upon the *King*. Following his gaze, he was clearly in rapture at the beauty of the *Princess*.

The Angel's innocent smile turned black all of a sudden. Not one time did she look at me, or anyone else but the King. However, all at once she fell back out of the window as if on air and was gone. Though, nevertheless, so was I, for the *vortex* took me…

3

I was withdrawn to the garden once again, crackling and popping amid the centrifugal storm.

The sky was that same orangey purple from whence it had been a couple of hours before. Though, quickly, reds of every hue were splattered upon all, bathing everything in a blood-red hue, signaling some sort of *Passover*.

I looked around and there was my *Celestial host,* standing just behind the four-foot in size boulder. She was back in statue pose and her hands were intertwined. The only way you could tell she was made of flesh was upon close inspection. I approached, and her eyes opened and followed me. This time being of a pale and peaceful quality albeit, still *macabre*.

"Greetings Archonian," I said. Her eyes were closed. Then, not knowing what to say next, I unconsciously began. "Why have I been brought here?"

Slightly raising one brow and after a stiff pause, *"I am not a keeper in the knowledge of all things."* Another short interlude and, *"you tell me. Why do you think you were brought here?"*

"I don't know. Ever since I have been here it has been nothing but darkness." She lightly raised her eyebrows once again.

"Darkness, you know that old man?"

"All too well."

"Give into the visions," she purred.

"Visions? Visions of death and dying?"

"*Dying*?" she asked. Still not moving, though her face was animated. *"Dying is why you are here, Artist,"* she said without emotion.

"I'm dead?" I asked, my voice growing smaller with each syllable. Gazing down at my hands I could see the familiar images on the top of each one. However, I also felt an immense longing, but for what? Some girl in my life? Something else I have failed to remember? Some unknown key to this gate that I have just misplaced and have yet to find again?

"Not yours Artist," she said without even opening her eyes. The garden took on a dank omnipresence that had a personality of all its own. The light was increasingly bruising the sky, the illumination being beaten darker reds and into a black cherry.

I was confused, and she continued, "You looked for it, and you found it. *Sometimes things should be left alone."*

"God damn it, I want some answers!"

"*AHHHH*" she dramatically screamed in my face. Hers, growing that terrible elongated version of itself. (Like as if you were to watch the pay-per-view channel without paying for it. It would appear all glitchy, interrupting the broadcast, though this was cleverly overcome with the use of just two strategically placed butter knives.) She didn't so much resemble a deformed mannequin, like a marionette being pulled away at a speed. This display had an accompanying augmented cacophony. Like the tormented screams of someone being murdered. Her entire demeanor changed. She sent me a vision of being burned alive that I started to ignite among the flames of a pyre that had engulfed my mind. The licking flames threatened to consume me with little hints here and there of the divine. Always just a pace ahead. Righteousness, being just out of reach, dangled before me.

Then, all was calm, and I was just standing in the same spot as before. Her celestial powers were limitless compared to my Earthly ones, being small charms and rituals. "*It is displeasing and a bit offensive Artist; none shall speak against thy host. My misguided feelings have caught chase ever and anon, lo, I have felt the vengeful wrath of a father's scorn. Sometimes,"* she paused as she searched for the right words, "*feelings can escape us, to seem things are one way, when in fact they are quite clearly another,"* she said, looking down at the grave, indiscretion eluding her.

She absentmindedly touched the spot over her breast with those long pale fingers. Then, as one resigned to the actions of having gone too far, she sent not a vision this time, but a feeling of such sorrow and verisimilitude, that simple punishment wasn't enough. A sadness was heavily bound upon her soul and I lost my breath just seeing this in my mind.

I suddenly felt extremely sick to my stomach and a weird detachment like that of a shadow or some misbegotten cadence had left a piece of something behind. Though, nevertheless, it was her that felt this way. She was sharing the experience of her pain with me. I began to dry heave and wondered if my mind had had enough. As she began to get closer to me, I felt only a dual harmony with her, still, as she approached, my blood quickened. More birds joined in the fray as others continued their agitated song.

"*Fear not Artist. Just remember, every decision you make is seen,*" she lowered her voice, "*Walk with me, for our journey shortly comes to an end, for soon.*" I accepted this and walked with her.

We traveled in silence for a moment, so I presently figured I would try to get down to the point and asked, "Can you at least tell me why I am here with you now?"

"I am to guide you to where you will see the brightest, most radiant light, that you have ever beheld."

"Speak Angel, so that I may understand, for if this is some sort of worldly lesson if that is the case, another way would have been more fitting."

Again, there was a moment of silence before the birds picked up their den. All the colors were almost bled out of the sky. Many stars could be seen. The wind started to put a chill in the air. I could hear birds chirping, and this gave me a pang of anxiety, which is often accompanied by a feeling of impending doom. She began; *"I am to guide you to the woman of suffering, though, I am not a keeper of knowledge in all things."*

"So, I am to be used as a puppet? What cruel game does your master wish to play with me?"

"*My master does not play games,*" she said coldly. *"I am to lead you,"* at this point, the den from the birds was becoming deafening. The Angel began to shutter and glitch in and out of existence, and the vision of her appeared and at once dematerialized. Repeating the process all over again.

The wind was growing stronger by the moment, the scent of *frankincense* filled the air.

"You haven't answered." I saw I had her attention. Slowly she turned to me. "Answer me one thing."

"What is it, Artist?"

"Where are you to lead me, and when?"

The Archonian Angel started levitating. Her voice was as if many, some low in pitch, some high, as if possessed. The sound of the birds was now an insistent scream, and the wind was violently threatening to knock my feet from beneath me.

Then, in a demonic voice she said, *"Be aware Artist, of your surroundings, for if I am to lead you to the brightest illumination that you have ever. beheld, you must be prepared. Be ready, in mind and spirit to receive the visions."*

The wind and the birds were unbearable, and she vanished amid the storm. She glitched right out of existence. Next, I was pulled within the tempestuous vortex. It was as if I was losing both mental and physical balance, albeit didn't matter because I lost consciousness.

4

I awoke next to a tree so I surveyed the area. Fog surrounded the field in front of me and queerly moved like a lost wraith or spirit among the damned to perdition. I wondered if the fog were souls caught in the vast expanse of limbo. The haunting consummation did not last long, for suddenly *Sol* crowned as photons of Ohr broke through the atmosphere, consuming the moisture of the specters, turning them into evaporating phantoms.

I was momentarily blinded by the light from a different direction. The quanta of illuminations began reflecting off the *monolithic obelisk.* From up here on the incline, the huge stone was at a height of sixteen to twenty feet tall, though, it was difficult to say for sure. Both parts were about half of their whole put together. I decided to go and investigate.

As I approached, I marveled at the polished surface, wondering what hand could have created such a smooth piece of art. Mostly though, I asked myself what it was for? I played with the idea that it may be a gateway of some sort and I may be able to get home through it. Again, I decided to rest, choosing the eastern side to sit on.

I got into a meditative position and tried to seal all the angel had said into my mind. Soon, I reasoned, my recent memories would return. Until then, I could barely hold open my eyelids, for they had gotten very heavy. I began to drift into sleep. A jolt rocked me back a moment later that must have been from my adrenaline.

As I considered these elements, I closed my eyes and fell into unconsciousness. I dreamt I was in an insane asylum, telling the workers that there was someone following me. Though, no one would believe me.

I awoke back in that strange room with the now smokeless hearth and sarcophagus. The old man was there, holding the secrets to this mess. His corpse growing colder and colder with every moment that thenceforth passed…

Chapter II
The guests have arrived

1

Meredith loved the old *Opera House*. She purchased it at a private auction five years ago.

Now, here she was, all this time later, still renovating it. Doing it by yourself was a long business though, nevertheless, it was also rewarding, in its aesthetic aspect.

Meredith was an attorney during the day, not of the domestic arguing type albeit mostly settling life insurance policies in small claims court. To forget all the former, during her leisure hours, she liked to play her violin. It was from the early eighteenth century. Purchasing it several years before the Opera House she was so particularly good at it. Even now, she was playing on stage the intro to *Antonio Vivaldi's* first act of *winter*.

One day, she mused to herself, she would be able to quit the firm and do what she loved the most. Though, for now, she would dream and play.

She went pealing through the opening notes. Just as she was beginning the first solo, she heard something being knocked over from the back of the auditorium. Seeing how there were only a couple of stage lights on, it was dark beyond the first few rows, she would have to go and make sure nothing was amiss.

After setting her violin down, she hopped off the stage in pursuit of the clamor. Another person in such circumstances might have been afraid of being all alone in such a big manor house all the time. However, of ghosts and phantoms she was not afraid. What did frighten her, was all that lurked just beyond the safety of the barred windows of the estate.

Saint Louis could be terrifying if you read or watched the local news for five minutes. Being from a bit further out in *Missouri*, she had read where even the locals claimed it was, and always *had*, a terrible reputation by way of its crime rate, civil unrest, and general city decay.

In addition to the dark, comes the lighted splendor of the old buildings. Mostly being from a revival era, when *America* went through a *neo-gothic* trend, from the late nineteenth century, lasting no more than around twenty years. Shortly thereafter, the style of the city saw a rebirth of the classical movement. Then, a few short years later, to keep up with the more modern culture, St. Louis started to build the more popular type of buildings that would come to dominate the landscape in years to come.

The more ancient parts of the city fall closer to the river, its old name being, *'The Nile.'* Furthermore, right across the said river, was *Egypt*, now called *Illinois*, after a native tribe.

They likened the *Mississippi* to the great river Nile for several reasons. The main one is that during principal settlement, as they were building up the area, they would send the tree logs by hand down the river. Workers were paid top wages at the time for building and moving on to just up the river, into Egypt.

In Illinois stands, some call America's first city: *Cahokia*. A small township best known first for its famous Native mounds. What's more, technically, the *Tumuli* or *Barrows*, are not at all in *Cahokia*. The main structure nonetheless. Being termed, '*Monk's mound*.' Also of note, is the singular train depot that is in Cahokia.

Throughout the 19th century, specialists have found, that most of the *'settlement hills'* were for burial. Over the years following, there have been rumors of demolishing the burial grounds in favor of an apartment complex. Anthropologists found good evidence to believe that the area was in the most recent capacity, before European settlement, was home to a *lunar blood cult.* Performing hundreds, if not thousands of sacrifices annually.

If the rain didn't come, human sacrifice. If it didn't get warmer, human sacrifice, all on the word of a primitive shaman. Also, cannibalism was practiced ever and anon among the natives.

Close by was the *'Cahokia Mounds Heritage Museum.'* Surrounding it on the land itself is the complete evidence of the practice of *lunar worship.* There is now, and has for centuries, stood a wood henge structure with its directions corresponding to the Moons cycles.

However, let me carefully turn your attention back to the old *'Monks Mound'* itself.

In the 20th century, a young archaeologist, *Edward W. Hook,* was granted authority to have a look around the famous settlement. While Edward had the fanciful idea that there was a hidden pyramid buried just beneath the gigantic *Tumulus*, he gathered all his savings from various resources and was able to secure a drill for the job. Though this drill was not of the contemporary household type, this one was for digging deep down within the Earth.

After going through all the requirements and recruiting several colleagues for the job, he began. Although, as he had been organizing, he had mistakenly overlooked that technically the owner of the barrows wasn't the state of Illinois. It was now the property of a *Father VenzVoss*, from Maryland. Well, after trying time and time again to reach the father, his requests were in vain, so he just moved on. That decision ended up costing him everything.

Seeming like he had only just begun, an insurance agency from Missouri came and conducted an inquiry into Edward and his team on the behalf of this Father VenzVoss, which came more like harassment. Demanding his findings, and forcing him to relinquish his Excavation after only three days, for bearing unfruitful results. His reason being, that just renting the machine for a week far surpassed his budget for the dig itself and he simply didn't have enough time to complete everything.

Three days and nothing. With funds depleted and this agent breathing down his neck, he was forced to shut down.

The local board, seeing his coming back empty-handed, quickly took back the temporary license to investigate the area and young Edward was devastated.

Now, two months later, Edward awoke after a dream that he was at the 'Monks Mound,' and an Egyptian pharaoh was chasing him and screaming. He surmised the Egyptian was yelling that he wanted his beating heart. Then, a moment later, he did not recall his dreams at all. The only thing he could think of was his passion for the *barrows*. He was pleased when realizing it was the weekend and he was off work and had no other plans. Today would be the day he would go back and check a few curious enigmas that the land had yet to reveal.

After making all the necessary arrangements, Edward headed out.

It was a bright day, and the clouds were as astonishing as the *Seven Spheres of, ZxTxS*. When he parked and made his way onto the main tumulus with all its steps, he was not in the least out of breath when he ascended to the top. The steps themselves were added around 1848 to 1850.

When he looked around, he saw that nothing had much changed in the preceding months since the dig. You could not even tell anyone had even been up here. The only difference was the regular trimming of the grass. From this vantage point, you can see the river itself.

Now, looking East, he noticed the other barrows all being illuminated by the noonday sun didn't have a shadow at all. Checking his watch, he noticed it was just past One O'clock PM.

Then, just out of the corner of his eye on the ground, something was shining. Damn near blinding.

Walking the yard or so to the spot, he kicked some brush away to reveal what was hidden before. Buried halfway down was a disk. He picked it up, noticing the heat that was radiating from it from being exposed to the sun. It had a strange-looking symbol on one side, the other was blank. Though, the polished metal itself was flawless, the inscription upon it was of machine-like quality and it was like nothing Edward had ever before seen. He ran his fingers the length of it. The steelmaking a slight hum with the movement.

He knew the first thing he had to do was have it examined by a friend of his from *'Saint Louis Medical University.'* Little did Edward know that day would alter the course of his entire future.

Meanwhile, Meredith was investigating the source of the clamor coming from the cupboards inside the old Opera House.

As she was passing the portrait of her grandfather, it had always reminded her of the stories, he had told her when she was little. Especially the ones about where he made his fortune, though the details were scattered and she could barely remember them. He was so mysterious to her.

Even now, looking at the old portrait of him that adorned the auditorium, he had that strange disk in his hand. He was staring at the viewer with that detached longing, they say it got worse after grandma died.

Entering the kitchen area, she went to flick on the lights but didn't get the chance.

"Boom!"

Meredith looked over to the counters and watched as two pans were being pushed out of the way and two of the biggest rats she had ever seen ran and jumped off the counter. One chasing the other.

She cried out. Then a moment later, she laughed and collected herself. There was talk of the place being haunted, well, at least that is what some people said in the comments section on the Internet. She found the little that she did know in the form of an article, that a very clever journalist had written that she stumbled upon when researching the estate.

The article was not exceedingly long though, it was interesting nonetheless. Some of the text explained that the last production that was advertised was from around ten years ago. It was about a strange phantom that haunted the Opera House. Though, at the same time, the said phantom was also playing the part of the Angel of music in the same cast.

Her grandfather oversaw the Opera House for forty years before his disappearance and given his age, his presumption of death. Though, at the time, she had no idea that this was the place she used to visit so long ago, for her mother had been estranged from her father for the better part of the last two decades.

In the preceding years after the purchase of the estate, her grandfather went on to author several books. During this time, he and his wife *Edna Maureen Hook* had a child. Though, the column didn't explain about her mother, *Claudia Rose*.

In a complete turn of events, Edward had single-handedly foiled an attack and apprehended the local murder suspect. Little was said about this, except that the man's name was *Ronove Shantell,* and he was found dead in his cell a day later. Being left alone he had managed to hang himself with a sheet tied to a set of bars.

Next, it read that after his wife had died several years later, the old man wasn't the same. One neighbor would go on to relate that, *'Edward was about all strange things after the Miss died. Always have some sort of motley people about the estate.'* What this meant, is your guess is as good as mine. Though mostly, the article read.' Little did they take seriously the fact that the newspapers were full of accounts of the very real monster in their midst, who had been caught by this man they were painting to be, *'Strange.'* The rest of the column being gossiped on the same things, and yep, also being paid for by a rival Opera house.

Naturally, when all the drama began it did nothing but get the theater extra publicity which was good for business. They had more seat sales than ever. The place was packed every night. Then, over the next few years, decreasing just a bit after two cinemas were built close by.

Quickly, she found different links to an incident where their daughter was a troubled teen and had gotten herself into a heap of problems, this she already knew, all too well.

Moving on, she quickly found what she was looking for. Yep, this was the right place she remembered coming to so long ago. Going back to the previous article, she looked closer for any details she may have missed.

That same, *'neighbor,'* related that, 'the rumors were, that even the gangs in the blocks surrounding the old Opera House, would avoid that part of the street.' The story was that one day after the Miss had died, the Mr. had brought her body back to life, for the Mr. was an author of strange books on ancient civilizations and other occult mysteries. A total of ten in all. Though the locals being ignorant of such ideas, were frightful of him.'

These same neighbors said that they had themselves seen the old lady looking out of the windows at night, waiting for someone to try to cross her husband. Well, besides the said *'Incident,'* there was not much more value from the article.

After the *'Incident,'* happened, Meredith's mother was having an increasingly tuff time staying in communication with the old man. Ever since Claudia Roses,' *Spiritual Awakening,'* or, *'accident,'* she was different they say, for it was when Meredith was too young to remember how it all had exactly happened.

So, one day, Claudia Rose had simply moved away. Later, as she was talking with Meredith, she informed her that her grandfather was dead. The revelation hit her hard because besides an uncle who was in a retirement home, she was left without relatives. Her father was hit by a drunk driver while he was on business one year her mother had explained, and that *'James,'* her, Claudia Rose's boyfriend, wasn't her father. That was fine though, she couldn't stand him, but tolerated him for mother.

As she started to get up, she saw someone standing next to the stage.

"*Hey*!" She cried.

It was a little kid around ten years old, a boy. She ran up to him. "*What are you doing in here?*" she asked in a stern voice, at the same time turning him around. At that moment, she saw a shadow of a man on the furthest back wall. Her heart sank to her gut.

"I thought I saw my brother and I found these," he handed her a set of keys.

"*Where did you get these?*" she asked.

"I found them in the front door." Immediately she remembered leaving them there because her hands were full when she returned home from work.

"Hey,' Meredith looked, and a little girl was coming up the aisle. "Come on Ricky," she said. "We have to go," the little girl yelled to her brother, not paying any attention.

"I thought you said it was your brother,"

"I don't have a brother, lady." He shook from her grasp. With her keys tightly in her hand, she let him slip away, watching the two children run up the concession aisle, they made a left at the threshold to the entrance. She heard the doors slam shut, rattling an old playbill that was hanging from an antique frame.

After, she made sure that the exits were securely locked and she put her violin away and decided to retire early. Even though she was off work the following day, she had lots of housework to get done.

2

Meredith's dreaming mind was full of scenes of medieval architecture. There were also people in a ballroom, all waving at her at the same time.

Once, her grandfather took her to *Venice* when she could barely remember. That was when Meredith's grandmother was still doing well, before all the doctors and the family arguments.

She could remember at night when she would stay with them sometimes, and her grandfather would read her bedtime stories. The tales of *Hamlet* and his three weird sisters she could remember well. There were other ones also. She had an especially vivid memory, from when she could have been no more than six or seven; it was the night of the *'Incident.'*

She was running through the gallery hall and a certain light was coming in the window from a streetlamp and the feelings it inspired to this day would bring her joy.

She would enter the kitchen and jump on grandfather's lap and Grandmother would be cooking something on the stove or the oven. *"Tell me again Grandpa?"* Little Meredith would ask.

"Which one this time?" He replied.

"The one, the one!" and she would shuffle around in his lap. *"About the cup and the angels!"*

"Oh, the grail, is it?" he asked.

"Yeah!"

"Once, there was a knight. A knight who was just returning from war, he found his sweet wife waiting for his honorable and regal return-."

"Ooo Wee,' Edward, now you tell the proper version." His wife would say.

"I'll tell my proper version," He replied a bit too sharply. "I mean, I will tell Meredith the real version." As he got to that last part, he started speaking in an elongated voice. Grandmother just smiled down at them. Then hearing something she turned, believing she had seen a shadow pass by the door, like an animal or something. The little girl noticed this as well but quickly looked back, dreamily listening to her grandfather as he told the story. "The French kings were descended from the long-haired Merovingians."

"What happened to the cups?"

"Well, it wasn't a cup. You see when Julian found-," he went on. Grandma was just now approaching the hall. She peeked out.

Nothing was there. Thinking she saw a cat's shadow or something of the like that got in last time, because things come up from the opera house side through the walls from time to time.

Upon reaching the landing, she noticed it was all dark except for a bathroom light that was on and one in the foyer downstairs. Then, standing at the top landing, watching down the gallery, she noticed Meredith's desk lamp come on. It was in the room they kept for her, across from the restroom.

Hearing a thud. This time though, there was an accompanying high-pitched squeal. She went back the way she had come. Going in pursuit of the sound, she thought that it was probably rats and most likely was not a burglar; bars on the doors and windows were a great investment for those latter kinds of pests.

The only real reason she had concern for alarm was because there was a serial killer on the loose. He had already killed several women in the neighborhood. The worst part was he broke into their homes and did unspeakable crimes to them before ultimately killing and dismembering them, and eating their parts. Even more chilling is that he drank all their blood. The papers called him, *'The Vampire Killer.'*

It seemed so humiliating for the police Meredith's Grandma thought. As she got further down the corridor, she grabbed the broom that she'd abandoned earlier in the afternoon.

Then, hearing Edward continue the story, she looked back at the way she had come.

It had been days since the last time she had caught wind of anything about the issue of any murderers or killings through gossip in the papers. To *Edna Hook,* until the person was caught, she considered them on the loose, even if it was a couple of weeks since the last happening. 'Ooh, Wee.'

Edna and her friends did not believe it when the papers would say that a killer had moved on. What about *Jack the Ripper* or *Zodiac*? They just bided their time, striking again whenever they chose. Least of all the neighbors, she thought as she carefully peeked out of the two-story window that was also barred like the rest of the manor. She wondered how they had installed them up here on the second story, outside.

It seemed like something horrible was always about anymore. What was the world coming to?

Before this last killer, there was a local man that had shot someone and said it was an *accident*. A bullet in the head is an accident? No not at all. Not to Edna. The suspect was buying a gun from a seller when the victim got shot and killed. Back to meet his maker. The worst part was what his momma went through. The courts just finished the case up recently. The man who killed him got ‘three years' probation. *Probation*, imagine that. *Probation* and *accidents*. 'Ooo wee,' she thought to herself. An accident. *Nah*. She did not believe that none of her *Red Hat Lioness* girlfriends did either. Though, it wasn't so strange, considering the suspect who got the probation had the same lawyer that they had gotten for *Claudia Rose*.

Now this other. This new evil. When it first got serious was when the two sisters went missing. When they never found them, many reports were looking for the boyfriends. Nothing from any of the calls and tips turned up any leads. All dead ends. Two solid months of investigations into the locals and still they yielded no results.

However, in a false lead, a man claiming responsibility in a letter to the local police department, stated that he had killed a prostitute in the *Washington Park* area and was wanted for questioning for the rape and murder of another. Later, they said that he had been stalking his last victim for a while. *'How long was a while?'* she asked herself.

Grandmother walked past the study on the right. The papers read that after raiding his house they found hundreds of notebooks of plans to do all sorts of unspeakable offenses to women the suspect knew. Offenses not just against the law, but the law of man as well. The things he admitted to doing to that first girl, *Jane Doe,* were all dismembered, he cut away every part of her and ate everything but the bones.

Edna shuddered as she walked into Meredith's bedroom, making sure everything was tidy. When she came to stay for the weekends, sometimes, the lights would just go on and off, though, when asked, Edward assured her it was due to the wires being crossed during installation. Even now, the light was on and the window was cracked. Looking around she noticed that the rocking horse was swaying back and forth. She stayed it with her hand and consciously gazed about the room. First going to shut the window that was cracked just a bit, the scent of barbecue was coming from one of the neighbors' properties.

Closing the window, and unbeknownst to her, a *shade* levitated just behind, through the highlighted glares of the windowpane, then backed up left and hovered to the right, and appeared to vanish.

She would have to remind herself not to leave the windows open so late in the evening; the nights were getting darker faster and cold drafts were liable to be the death of them before it was said and done.

Making sure everything was in its place, she backed up and out of the room and shut the door behind herself. Gazing down toward Edward and Meredith and hearing a giggle and Edward roar with the climax of the story, she silently smiled.

The ominous grandfather clock at the other end of the hall began to tick its tock of the hour. At once, noticing that the bathroom light was also on, she crossed the corridor and went inside.

It smelled like bleach and other chemicals. Edna, gazing into the antique mirror of the medicine cabinet, then to the toilet and mused, *'I might as well go now since I'm already here.'* Seeing a glimmer albeit not being receptive to the physics involved, the mass in the bathroom corner started to quickly levitate towards her. It materialized right before her and she was so startled that she let out a shriek.

"Ahhh."

She was terrified by the form that it took, though; just as shocking were its eyes on her. They seemed so warm, yet murderous. At that moment, from across the threshold, it came on a collision course, right for her. As the specter slammed into her she thought, *'could ghosts touch people?'*

She hit the wall, losing consciousness. Luckily for her the bathroom door slammed shut as well. The mass just levitated above. Though strangely, it seemed to be protecting her.

3

One of the two intruders had slicked-back hair and was a complete monster in comparison to the manifestation that was lurking about. He clicked a zippo to light an unfiltered cigarette. The smell instantly filled the downstairs living room at the Opera House.

Getting through the bars of the front door was nothing for the two criminals. The ghost came down the steps and upon seeing them, vanished through the wall, leaving vapors of smoke on the exterior. The shorter of the two men went in pursuit and disappeared within.

Meanwhile, on the second story in the bathroom, Edna was pulling herself up off the floor. Her nose was bleeding and her elbow hurt from the fall. Trying the doors handle did little good, for it didn't even have a lock.

It was jammed. Her arm protested its use. *'Well fuck,'* she thought.

She was bound within.

Then, someone was violently pushing the door in, from without.

4

Edward first heard something slam violently hard in the hallway. A moment later, Grandmother screamed.

"Grandpa, what is that?"

"Them damn rats again," he said, as he picked her up and took her to the adjoining bathroom that was between bedrooms. Then, setting her down, he said, "be a good girl, and Grandpa will bring you a sweet back."

"And finish the story?"

"And also, finish the story. Now do what I said." They had practiced this labor several times in case of emergency. Closing the door, he used a key to lock it from the inside. At once, switching the bedroom light off, Edward closed his eyes and listened with not just his ears, but his mind.

"Boom!" It sounded like someone had flipped over the dining room table. He stood completely still and silent, appearing to be listening and just a moment after, he stepped outside of his physical body and into the *Astral*. He just walked through the wall, as his physical body was still in the bedroom, in the dark.

5

Meredith the dreamer, was starting to stir in her sleep, like she was running from something. Some endless void with a vast abyss beneath, dragging her down deeper and deeper, and she just couldn't seem to escape.

All this memory, or dream, coming through as a vision, from her subconscious. Then, her breathing returned to normal.

6

When Edward got onto the hallway gallery, he could see there was the essence in the bathroom and three downstairs, just seconds away from coming up here.

As he started to make his way down to his wife, *he*, in this *astral state*, pulled the disc out from his pocket and gently, with the other hand's forefinger, traced the edges of the *pentagram*. Then, connecting the lines that met in the middle formed the outer rings of the intricately carved details.

Saying the proper emanation names, *"TxSZxT, Ashur, XsTzX."*

Time, to a minor degree, slowed. At once, it was as if he were floating underwater, both in sound and insight.

The grandfather clock in the upstairs foyer slowed to a halfway tick-tock, as it proclaimed the hour. He sprinted down to where his wife was. Trying the handle, he realized it was jammed. He almost got in when he felt the *'criminals,'* on their way up the stairs.

Whoever stepped onto the landing from the steps would encounter first, that bedroom he had accidentally left open. Beyond that, was his mortal shell, and beyond that, was Meredith, awaiting his return.

7

Meredith, from the present, started to toss and turn. In the room, she was bathed in darkness, but if you were in it and embraced it for long enough, it became a deep blue and would yield unknown secrets to the steady gaze of the voyeur held enrapt.

A figure walked past once, then twice, and the door was opened all the way seemingly by its own accord. In the inky blackness, it was hard to make out what physical properties the figure held.

"Click, click, click" of boot heels. At this, Meredith's sleeping figure started to stir.

He walked into the room before him. Around the man was a vaporous smoke, almost appearing like big snakes. Coiling out and around his back, only made of smoke wraiths.

He had been here before, he thought. The place had changed little.

That could hardly be said of himself. He was almost one of them now. That place had a way of working its little magic on everyone who set foot on that damn land. What about it has the power, to obsess one so?

The smoke that continuously followed him was crowded with faces. Some in agony, others say in pleasure. They appeared, and once again, vanished, just to reappear into a new expression of terror and pain. He hit his cigarette, the cherry lighting the whole room up as he did so, sending the smoke demons into a new frenzy.

He made a circuit about the room. As he approached her, she was lying face up. Looking like the perfect broken doll. Then, putting his opposite cigarette hand over her mouth about an inch and looking closer, he saw she was nude under that fold in the sheet. Her visage reminded him of the statue, *'The Ecstasy of Saint Teresa,'* by that *baroque* sculptor *Bernini*. She was on her back with her breast poking out. Her belly and the pubic area were shaved to a landing strip. He threw down his cigarette and smashed it on the floor with his boot. The shadows fell back as the smoke kicked up a new *maelstrom*. Licking his fingers, he ran them through his greasy hair. Licking his middle finger as he approached her.

Something caught his attention before he got the chance to see what was inside. The shadows were playing tricks on him again. That's what going from one world to another did though, it messed with your mind. He put his hand over the other one that was held above her mouth and nose. He mentally started to peel back the types of *plasma* and *false strings,* up, up, and around his hand, as he whispered the words that he had learned from that old bitch from the swamps in *Andalusia.* She had shown him things that he never would have dreamt of knowing growing up on *Ha-Aretz* as a *Daywalker*, let alone witnessed as a *Demu* in that land of crossroads. That once thought to be inaccessible *dementia* that yet proved attainable through various disciplines.

Meredith awoke in the present and couldn't move; sleep paralysis had deeply set in.

8

Edward's essence followed the sound of the voices down the steps; they were just on the first landing.

Time, for the magician, was still moving incredibly slow; going quickly down the hall he levitated right before them.

One was a human, a killer by the smell of him, a murderer of innocents. This was the killer from the papers that was being reported about seemingly for days and nights now, scaring the hell out of all the women in the area, sending them into a panic and murdering the rest.

'It could have been Edna you bastard,' Edward's incorporeal form thought, as he levitated without them knowing. One of many lessons his old sage had taught him.

The same could not be said of the second intruder; it was of Earth though, and was human. It was a *Daemon* of some sort, that strange mixture of the dual spheres. He was telling the other where to go, even now he was saying, *'bathroom.'*

Edward had to choose, and fast. Re manifesting, then, once again, was back in his body and he knelt, pulling out a pistol that was strapped to his ankle.

"Click," the safety switched off. Then, walking to the threshold of the door and now back inhabiting his mortal body, he looked at the grandfather clock and willed time to recur back to normal. No sooner had he willed it than it was so. Reality quickened back into step. He had a moment of disorientation, then collecting himself, he caught the two just as they got halfway up the last set of stairs leading to the landing.

"Boom! Boom! Boom!" One of his bullets had missed. As soon as it went past, the manifested *demon* and his smoke wraiths vanished. The other bullet hit the hand that the *Demu* that had his weapon out. The next shot to go off was from that one, hitting Edward just above the bicep on his left arm.

"Boom! Boom! Boom!" Edward shot off three more rounds. All but one found their mark, hitting the trespasser in each leg.

Edna was panicking in the bathroom. She had almost passed back out from hyperventilation when she finally stood looking into the mirror, it was, no, it could not be him. Why was she seeing her husband but older in the glass?

Edward, after letting his wife out of the bathroom, retrieved young Meredith as well. When he saw he could not remedy the situation without making sure it was never to happen again, he handed young *Meredith* to *Grandmother* and explained to her he was going to wait out in front of the authorities. Then, he went to question the killer alone, in a large converted hallway closet.

Once inside, realizing that he knew this man, remembered that he was here not so long ago. When asked why he was there and a dozen other questions, no revelations were forthcoming at first.

Then he told. He told it all, even some lies. He burned the violators face badly with his full pack of cigarettes. Each one, he slowly put out. One at a time.

It took the police half of an hour to respond. They said it took so long because it was a Friday night. When they got there, with Grandmother's account of what happened along with little Meredith's, that's all they needed. Though, they did want to speak with her husband and had a search team scouring the neighborhood for the culprit. Then, while finishing the questioning, everyone's attention was stolen away as a commotion down the hallway was apparent. Next, in a climactic moment, out from around the corner of the dining room came the murderer.

"Please help me," he pleaded in a foreign voice, thick with accent.

One of the cops pulled out his gun and yelled, *"freeze,"* and one of his partners intercepted the fleeing man. With one fluid motion, a deputy used the man's weight against himself and sent him crashing down with all his momentum to the floor. The girls both screamed and then the remaining officers were on top of him.

Then, the old man came out of the darkened room. The same deputy that pulled out his gun, once again yelled, *"hold it."*

"Grandpa!"

Edward slowly walked into the room. It was as if a record had come to a reeling stop suddenly when he entered.

"Edward!" He looked the part of an evil mage—hooded robe on. Eyes reeling and feigned resistance to all. They all looked at the wound and his arm laying there lifeless. Blood was dripping in fat drops off his index finger.

"I've been shot," he said with a look of confusion. Meredith began to scream.

9

The present-day Meredith was also screaming, though this time she was wide awake.

It was still dark out, that much she could tell by looking through the crack in the shutters. However, the subtle signs of illumination of the coming dawn were sending shades and specters every which way, recreating all that was into what all that shall ever be.

Chapter III
Inquisitional Torture Devices

1

After putting a fire on from the remains of a pile of unevenly cut wood that I found I wondered as to who had acquired them, for whoever had, had gouged them out of the tree. Almost it seemed, they took the chunks out a bite at a time and this is what they had spat into the bundle. The date on the package that the logs had originally come in read over five years ago.

After removing the screen from the hearth, I found some old lighter fluid and sprinkled a bit of it in. Next, grabbing the poker that was in the shape of a pitchfork, I began pushing the contents around. The ceiling was quite high from the spin of the vault, but still, there were no windows to be seen. Looking around and figuring the previous occupant wouldn't mind me snooping around a bit, I followed along the walls and eventually found a bathroom. It seemed to be the most modern embellishment that decorated this place. Looking back across the chamber, into the chair with the lion's feet and there was the crypt's last resident. Gone now. It seemed a shame, the old hermit, in retrospect, fit the part for sure of a *'Moses'* archetype. Again, surveying the ceiling, it did appear like a movie set, even him. However, everything was very authentic, it was just that he seemed so out of his time and melancholy. Well, I thought, 'I seemed to fit right in here then.'

As I approached the desk, the digital clocks analog numbers were displaying three thirty-one am. It was blinking a vivid cool blue. Picking up a brass hourglass and examining it, I turned it upside down. Grabbing the set of car keys and next to those were two weathered tomes and some writing implements. Also, a leather pen case. Then, taking a closer peek inside there was a small handgun. It looked to be a .380. I own one, I think. Or did. Additionally, I was trying to find a calendar, or better yet, a phone and I wondered who I would ring had I the device to do such.

Unhooking the clasp on the first book, I quickly realized it was a handwritten grimoire. This triggered my memory and I thought, *'where were my journals?'*

Going over to the antique sofa, I looked in my bag. *'Damn, they weren't there.* As I tried to focus my attention on remembering, I was once again filled with that longing. That imperceptible feeling of panic that threatens to consume one when they must accept their lot in life is not what they had expected. More times than not, it's a pitiful sight, being resigned, when all you want to do is have everything be normal again. I put the pistol into my bag and went back over to the desk, the second book was a Log Manuscript of, *'The Patriarchs of the Eternal Flame,' Volume One and Volume Two.'* Interesting, must be rare, for I had never read nor heard of such a text.

"Bang!" something fell off a bookcase that I hadn't noticed, for everything was slightly cramped. Instantly, going over to the baroque bookshelf, I quickly scanned the catalog. I realized the old man had a veritable goldmine, in just a few of the grimoires alone.

Seeing my movements in that mirror, again I gazed deep within, locally for the first time, taking in the contents of the entire room. Quickly, I saw that I hadn't observed several things until now.

There was an abacus to the left of the chair with the lions' feet and from the ceiling as before, though now I perceived some cords, exposed going through the wall, beyond the sarcophagus. There seemed to be an ever so slight vapor radiating from that display of the medieval iron maiden.

As I went to examine the inquisitional torture device, I almost tripped on an old leather-bound portfolio. It was a heavy volume of exquisite workmanship and design.

Picking it up with a grunt, I set it on the desk. Seeing it was of the type that to upend it, one had to release it by a piece of leather cord. I unwound it three times. It groaned in protest at being unbound. The first passage was in dedication, it read:

'This photo album is bequeathed to Edna Maureen Hook.
'

In a gold leaf typeset, that was enclosed in an ornamental frame.

Then, directly under that handwriting, was another passage. It read:

"Congratulations, my sweet daughter, I hope a family of your own, leaves you complete."

That was nice. This Edna must have gotten this as a gift, at her wedding, from her mother. Turning to the next page, there was indeed a wedding photo, it was in black and white. It was of a young man and a pregnant woman who was shoving cake into his mouth and looked like he had already gotten it all over hers. Both were laughing, and the rest of the people were also in a joyous constitution.

Over the next few pages, the rest of the ceremony commenced. Then, abruptly the images were scattered over the next few years and they had the baby. It was a girl. The photo album progressed in years and quality. There were also trinkets here and there and some stamps and a birth certificate.

Then, the content switched dramatically. The girl became a woman and before long the parents were seeing her off to school. There was an article from a newspaper where the man in the photo was a part of the unveiling of an ancient town center in Greece. This same young man, after returning home, had an excavation himself, though it was a bit more local and it was long before he had gotten married. He was much more dramatic appearing back then, it seemed. He had authored a book about the place where he held his anthropology investigation, it was called *'Secrets of the Mounds.'* Then, the content switched to playbills from an opera house.

Turning the page once again, there was this same man after he was married and in front of a medieval castle and a machine-like person was waving to the photographer. The man was with some priests of some denomination or another. *'Holy shit,'* I thought.

On the next page, the original mistress of the photo album grew into a distinguished lady. Here she was surrounded by others who wore one of the most absurd matching hats I had yet to behold.

On the next page were assorted images of the man *Edward Hook.* He was a part of a lodge and was surrounded by other distinguished men of a like nature covered with society patches and sashes.

The rest of the album was scattered, mostly images of the lioness, sinking deeper and deeper into an age of declamation. She was alone in most of the photos' but smiling at the camera. It must have been this Edward Hook guy taking the pictures.

Next, several blank pages were yellowed with age.

I carefully closed the book, rewound it, and put it back on the shelf from whence it had fallen. Putting my hands on the desk wondering why the tenant of the room had locked himself away in here, though more importantly, why was I even here?

I was feeling tired once again, so I instinctively stretched and in so doing turned my body just the right way to where I found myself once again looking into that scrying mirror. I surveyed all the objects in the room. My attention was once again drawn to the sarcophagus with that barely perceptible vapor that was still coming off it. I made my way around the room to look it over more fully. Hopefully, it wasn't poison or gas of some kind.

Approaching it, I saw it was a few inches taller than me and was exquisitely carved. I ran my fingers along the front of the smooth edges. It must be in dedication to a Pharaoh.

The Egyptian coffin was fully adorned with hook and flail. Each hand, in turn, had crosses along the outer edges where hieroglyphics were carefully etched on the sides that ran in intricate cartouches.

Running my fingers along with the characters, the symbols told the story of a girl who was raised in the ways of the Pharaohs at the Temple of Isis. Upon their deaths, the inhabitants would be reborn, though only after their personal forty-two confessionals and *Opening of the Book.* Feeling, further along the text, it explained that before you are reborn, you must traverse the *du 'at.*

"Ehhh," my finger was pricked. *"Fuck!"*

Great, that's all I need out of this confusion, a paper cut to get infected and rot my damn finger off. As I instinctively put it to my lips—a big drop of blood splat on the floor in front of me, then another.

"Damn," I said to myself as the blood hit the marble ground.

Then, a curious thing happened. The blood, instead of drying, pooled together and ran along a small crack in the surface that was in the slab on which I currently stood. The blood dripped into a barely perceptible fissure within the sarcophagus. I got down on my haunches to investigate further.

Gently, I pushed on the tomb's bottom stone.

Nothing. Then, giving it another push, -

-nothing still.

There was more writing running along the base of the supporting stone, from whence it stood.

It was written in ancient Latin.

"Per me transitis in urbem vae;
Per me transis in aeternum dolorem;
Per me in plebe perdita.
Iustitiae mee conditor fabricae movescit;
Me numinis alere munus erat;
Summa sapientia, primaque caritas.
Ante me nullae sunt res, nisi res
Aeternus, aeternus, i sustineo.
Spes omnis qui huc intratis deserite."

I knew the significance of the words at once. Though, I'm no expert, I am learned in some of the more dead languages. It was from a translation of one *Reverend H.F. Corey,* who at the time, had deciphered the text and in so doing coined the less commonly used phrase from *Dante's* epic poem, *'The Divine Comedy.'*

In English, it read:

"Through me, you pass into the city of woe:
Through me you pass into eternal pain:
Through me among the people lost for aye.
Justice the founder of my fabric mov'd:
To rear me was the task of power divine,
Supremest wisdom, and primeval love.
Before me things create were none,
save things Eternal, and eternal I endure.
All hope abandon ye who enter here."

It was above the entrance to Hell.

The passage reminded me not only of *'Inferno,'* but also of an essay I recently read while researching the legend of the *'Holy Grail,'* that many experts have an opinion on what this physical object was, or was not.

Let's look at it as an *'idea,'* from which many scholars of long repute have spent hundreds of years deciphering its riddles and mysteries, all in search of its glory and the knowledge of it. One of the proverbial *Philosophers Stones.*

In this text, there was a *Templar* that upon their end, knowing full well they would be betrayed, had taken this *'idea,'* to France. Though some say a completely different place, called Andalusia, and eventually died and was buried in his crypt. The former place was put along with such ranks as *Atlantis* and *Lemuria.*

To keep tomb robbers from misappropriating the corpse, the guardians had the actual coffin and remains inside of an *Iron Maiden,* that was also in the said tomb. The same medieval torture devices were used here, to make sure this most honorable and *Holy Knight* of the *Temple* wasn't disturbed, for his remains were in the tunnel, bound within the earth. Though, also in this legend, a clever detective stumbled upon the clockwork alchemy to unlock the device.

That reminded me of something.

I do remember seeing a Templar pen, on the man from the photo album. In that same thesis about the Grail, it explained that in these dynasties there was a society of mason-like archetypes that as an added security from tomb robbers, created their form of the iron maiden. The ones they used were copper for alchemical reasons. To penetrate the contents therein, one would just have to look along the inner side of the flail and I suppose, the one I got pricked with and there should be a small lever on the underside. I felt along the length of it.

Nothing.

I was already on my haunches, and feeling with my fingers along the exterior right side of the sarcophagus. As I gently pulled there was a click from inside the device. Slowly, it started what I can only describe as *unwound.*

"Click. Click. Click!"

Damn, it was slow.

Presently it opened, and the Egyptian pharaoh imparted the secrets it was holding within.

A fog emitted from the bottom and there was a huge turn wheel, like the ones used in bank vaults. I pushed as hard as I could and to my surprise, it worked. The mechanism within started to kick into gear. Then, as if a vast engine suddenly came on, the heavy steel door adjusted itself, then started to withdraw within. Smoke came out of two hoses in a hydraulic burst of steam.

Once the gate had cleared out of my present course, I stepped into a very dark corridor with a barely perceptible light at the end. As my hand guided me, I seemed to have touched many crawling things. I came to realize I was passing many rooms; just being absent of light. I knew, on instinct, to stay as far back away from these as possible.

Many strange things must have been behind that first one, for I noticed it sounded like huge chains being thrown about inside and the handle of the door was brass with a bloody handprint adorning it. Like as if that were the code or password to get in. The reason I mention it is because of the way they were being dropped, then dragged. As if something was being led along, just to be yanked back down again.

The second one, sounded like they were fighting dogs inside, causing me to walk away in repulsion, for it sounded like the voices of men were betting on the beasts and it made me want to burn the place down. That one was not hard to pull myself away from, I hate that shit. The third one had, it sounded like, a crowd of girls playing together. I mean, women you could tell that was in ecstasy. That was the most difficult one, I must admit, to pull away from.

The fourth one sounded like an argument between a man and a woman. Some of the things that were being spoken to each other were horrible. Not being so many curses as, *confessions*. This was as bad as the rest of this nightmare of a corridor I currently found myself in.

Finally, I was at the end. I heard a deafening roar as I wrenched the exit open. As if by pulling on it had triggered the rest of the doors to all be opened at once. I could only imagine the fate of the women in ecstasy. Who knows, maybe that would be a fitting end though, I wasn't going to wait to find out.

Escaping at last and slamming the door shut behind me, it sounded like something as big as a horse crashed up against it. Falling into the alley, I soon realized, I was in the back of the biggest house I had ever seen.

2

I laid there for a moment, then realizing the streetlights were on and it was the dead of night, I got up.

Carefully surveying the area, I saw movement, and to not draw attention to myself, I looked away, as two very suspicious persons walked between the houses, then vanished.

I took in the whole back part of the estate, which I could only assume was a mansion of the most haunted classical variety, it was astonishing. I backed up to account for both properties on either side in comparison. The Mansion was much older and twice as big as each on either end.

Out of the corner of my eye, I noticed the same two individuals were making another circuit around the house opposite. Then, the back porch of that same house's screened-in back door screamed as it was opened, slamming shut a moment later.

"Renee Eyyyy. Slap!"

Seeing it all in the reflection in the glass from the electric meter, I acted like I was busy working on a task. About a minute later an elderly man came hobbling off of that same back porch.

He babbled his way into the alley behind me.

"But. But. Hayley. Hayley. Hey," he yelled.

I played to ignore him, fidgeting with some tools. Carefully, I began sliding a screwdriver up my sleeve.

Hearing the back door to the old man's house being yanked open again from within.

Then, from the back porch, the younger man called, *"Granddad, what are you doing out here?"*

The grandson seemed more aggravated than angry, as if this were a completely normal thing for the old man to do.

"No. No. No one's supposed to be in that house," he said. Feeling like I had to interact now, I turned to address the situation.

"Hello there," I said, trying to cheer the mood but his stare was ice cold and glaring through me.

"No one's supposed to be in, there."

"Sir, I'm sure you are mistaken. That may have been the previous owner, but I assure you, Mr. Um, Hook. Mr. Hook put me in charge, just before he, um, left."

"Is that right?"

"Actually yes. I live here now and have managed to lock myself out." I lied, though, a little nervousness escaping. Still, he looked through me, sensing my deceit. I knew it.

"You calling me a liar boy?" he said. All traces of the elderly old man evaporated with the fog that started to surround him. I looked over and the man that was still on the porch was now joined by a pregnant woman who wore a menacing look on her face and piercings on her lip and nose.

Out of seemingly nowhere, two guys tried to jump me from both sides. I fell back out of the way and they both violently crashed into each other. As they tried to grab me, their momentum doing the rest of the work.

Then, the old man's face turned into something, that seemed beyond me. The strange thing was, my mind resisted, making sense of what it had become, or what it didn't become. All I know is, I couldn't tell if it was a wolf or an owl or strangest of all, a hairless pale thing that was in stark contrast to the being that first approached me just a moment whence. The creature the old man was becoming's eyes shone like a *reptilian*. I was pulled into them.

I saw myself being extracted out of my skin, then siphoned through a wormhole that could traverse all external realities, that were collectively known as, *'The Dementia.'* Then, with a vision of the Archonian, I struggled to free myself of this enchantment, being fueled by anger now. His spell being broken, someone grabbed me from behind by my shoulders. This time they connected their assault though, luckily for me they were weak and I lightly spun them around.

It was the pregnant girl from the porch. Then, someone grabbed me from either side. I was held fast struggling but still bound.

In a macabre moment, the woman looked slightly up at me and then her body broke like a marionette's mannequin and everything begat that stop motion quality as in the garden.

"Click, clock. Click, clock."

With a malevolent grin, the pregnant demons' eyes began glowing, like two burning coals of brimstone.

"Do you wanna see my baby?" She said, in an innocent voice.

"What?"

"I fucking asked, if you wanna see, ma baby?" She screamed the last part. Spittle flying in the streetlight. The night sky started to give birth to the dawn's earliest photons, kissing the atmosphere in its promise of coming illumination. The man holding my left arm started to giggle ignorantly.

"Show me. Show em all o' baby."

"All o' baby," the old man joined in the surreal madness.

"Yeah, yeah! *Show em, da baby,"* the smallest of the attackers demanded.

She pulled up her shirt, revealing two swollen breasts. Green infection leaked out and down her abdomen and she had a very wet appearing rash. Among it all was a boil and big black spots on the flesh of her chest, exuding a type of oily slime. Next, I got to her stomach.

The *'baby,'* in question was staring directly at me from the woman's belly. In likeness, it was that of the old man, and or, the older brother. Same cats' eyes. The only difference was, had it not been for the resemblance being attached to this woman and himself, it would appear not to be a baby at all. Nothing even human. Well, in the normal sense of the word.

It was some sort of alien type of *arachnid.* Beside the grotesque face, protruded two long legs from each side of the creature's head. Clear slime was drooling from each of its arms, crust coming off like snow where it had dried.

Starting to cry, its arms began animatedly moving.

They all started to laugh, especially the old man.

"Ode 'em," she ordered. They complied. That's when I heard one of the men say it.

Said that word.

The name of that place. Everything seemed too slow.

"What did you say?" I asked the tormenter to my right.

"Andalusia. Andelijia, *Andalusia.*"

"You," she screamed, getting the man's attention. *"You shut your fuckin mouth."*

"Ya' Quinta," he answered, shaking his head up and down.

"What the fuck is wrong with you people?" I said, I had assumed to myself, but the demoness picked up on it.

The woman at once snapped back.

"What da fuck is wrong with us? What the fuck, is wrong with you?" She screamed.

"Nothing as serious as I thought, because you all, *are some sick fucks!"*

"A snow, for dat, is going to make youse, eats, my, pusay." At that, the company started to historically laugh again, and a white discharge came out of their mouth from the face in her stomach. It was the color of infection.

She approached, all the time pulling down the dirty sweatpants she wore, baby screaming bloody death.

I braced myself as I saw a flash.

It was like a lightning bolt went off, and I happened to grab at it with both hands at the same time. I was thrown amidst a vortex. This one though was unlike the perpetual knots that were made and then unmade by the *Oreads*. That was the last thing I remember before I lost consciousness…

3

I woke up in the garden once again and there was only one thing I could honestly think of.

It was her.

What was it I felt for her? Compassion, eh, a bit, sure. Lust, eh, a bit of that too. I would try to unravel it all when the dust settled.

First, to understand what was going on, I had to understand, her. For, since I can remember, she is the only soul in the last day that didn't want to kill me or who wasn't already a corpse.

As the morning bloomed, I could just make out two of the biggest trees that I had ever seen in the distance. There appeared a lake, that was running betwixt the two-dominating conifer amidst this savage garden, where I found myself.

There was a patch of mysterious fruit, outside of the Angels grove and it looked so good. I had to try one. Then my mouth started to water and I had a terrible thirst. I picked up one of the strange fruits and pulled it from the stalk, cracking and popping loudly as I disconnected it.

Being about the size of a banana, they grew in shape into a bloated swollen thing. Kidney in form and growing in rows, sort of like pumpkins.

Squeezing on it a bit, I realized it wasn't too hard, like an orange with skin like an apple. I squeezed it a bit harder and pushed my fingernail tip-in. It at once responded to the pressure and out came a couple of small tears of juice. Then, smelling the liquid that was now running down my hand, I realized it was a bit sticky. I touched my tongue to it. It wasn't bad at all. I pushed the top layer of the skin off and smelled the inner part. It seemed fine, so I sank my teeth into it.

It was amazing. I pictured myself growing fat on these bleached white fruits. I sat there and gorged myself for around twenty minutes.

As I was sitting there with the strange fruit in hand, I had the strongest feeling I was supposed to be waiting for the Angel to show me my destiny or some greater purpose. Contemplating the Archonians' nature, I instinctively got up and made my way over to the small glade where I had first encountered her.

I sat cross-legged beside the memorial rock and closed my eyes to meditate on what this could all be about. I began to feel very drowsy from the strange fruit and I dozed off.

During unconsciousness, I saw people dying and the city burning. The Angels, well, Archonians, were in battle against these, *'Others.'* The *Qulophians* from the *nine southern spheres.* A grandfather clock was there ticking, and then that damn serpent consuming bodies and keeping their souls bound.

I jolted awake to find it had only been a few moments, so I stretched out on the grass, burying my arms at the base of the big rock. Next, everything seemed to evaporate, and it was like a blanket of fog enveloped me.

4

Then, once again, I was on that battlefield, the smoke filling the sky in big gulfs going past. This time though, I had my Archonian Angel with me for protection.

It was crazy the amount of chaos that was going on around me. One man, impaled by an incredibly long sword as he spat a dark curse into his deliverer's face as he was dispatched. Over there, two men were shouting, one had a crossbow and a group was advancing on more knights that were approaching from the right-hand side. Next, several men surrounded them. Off to my left three others were about to spring on an unfortunate warrior. For, he was twice as big as them and they both still looked nervous.

The first one sprang into action, making a circuit around him, his companion didn't think twice, running up and stabbing him in the ribs with a short dagger as soon as he turned to watch his own back.

The first companion attacked with a steel mallet; it knocked the poor fellow's helmet in and in effect, it peeled the front of his forehead right off. Grey matter looking like ground-up beef, vomiting out of his forehead.

Then, there were three on one, the first knocking a lone champion over the head. The other man hitting him from behind in the back with a mase. The hidden companion of the others sprang up and stabbed him in the gut when he was already done.

This was a horrible sight.

I felt like a piece of shit just bearing witness. When I thought I had all that I could take of these sights, I saw the *King* himself being surrounded by two formidable-looking assassins. The gigantic fellows knew their business, bounding forward through the shouts and thick smoke coming from an infernal wagon close by.

Attached to the wagon was a magnificent steed. It was still tied to the reins, struggling to free itself. Pulling it seemed, with everything it had and in so doing, knocked itself down in the process. The flames started to lick at the beast, almost upon it.

Grunting once again with the effort, it got back up and pulled its head in such a way that it freed itself, wood splinters and leather cords flying in every direction, though, it had only escaped the consuming flames to be challenged by a great *Nefilei*. The warrior giant let out a barbarous scream as he charged at the horse, but it was faster than lightning and kicked him square in the face. At once reminding me of the strange fruit.

It truly was a magnificent creature I thought as it flexed its thunder among this storm. Then, it slowly stepped on its fallen opponent and trotted off in the opposite direction. My vision was obscured as the horse went on its way.

Hearing a fresh clamor from behind, turning, I saw another group getting ready to mob upon a lost soldier. At this point, the chaos was so thick that it was hard to tell who was on whose side.

A new group was trying the same routine as the other infantry. One of their numbers going in, his armor screaming with the effort.

That's when he fell over. Arrow sticking out of the back of his neck, just between his helmet and steel plate at the nape. To the right of that fallen Knight, a great tree of a man was sizing up his next competitor. Laughing, the other just looking intently ahead, as if he could have stood a chance. A seasoned warrior came in to deliver the killing blow behind the *Nefilei*. Before the ax could connect though, another of the giants charged the first in line, screaming at the top of his lungs, it would have cut him straight in half had it not been for his armor. Therefore, he subsequently, pushed in his helmeted head, bending his clavicle to the breaking point. It bent and then collapsed under the hit. Malevolently, the Great Nefilei stopped, and licking the sword in a mad fury he charged the remaining knight as fast as he could, being cut down several feet beyond by a fallen enemy, determined to take someone else to *Hell* with him.

Meanwhile, the Kings Assassins were ready to advance now that he was on his own.

The first one to come in had courage for sure albeit in this world courage fell short to a seasoned scrapper such as himself. He followed the man's movements with lightning-quick speed, then parrying the mobster's weight back onto his arm and in one fluid motion, flipped him forward and onto his back. Dust went everywhere as he fell with a heavy thud. Though, the warrior quickly realized the King hadn't let go of his arm. He bent it to one side against his knee, cracking the bone and then breaking it with another sickening pop. The man let out a torrent of curses.

The Imperial Monster wasn't finished yet. Pulling out a dagger from his boot and then a heavy cloud of smoke obscured the figures for a quarter of a second. All that could be seen were great arches splashing to and fro. Standing up and walking forward with the bloodlust upon him, the Kings carnage had given birth to his old enemy, *Pride*.

That seemed to be who he was truly at battle with here today.

The King, locking eyes with his next victims, two companions, stranded from the rest of their mob. The Red Stained King began to maniacally laugh to himself.

From another battle just to the left, a shield came crashing in on another unfortunate fellow's skull who was about to defeat an opponent, hitting him square in the temple, crushing the bone.

He toppled over into a heap.

Then, another assassin approached the King. This time brandishing a whip. *"Slash! Jerk!"* The Imperial Monster was faster than the eye though, somehow, he had caught the assassin's whip around his own wrist and was pulling him forward. As he approached, he smacked the barbarian in the mouth, in midair. When he landed, the King dispatched him with the same short dagger to the man's chest, effectively, piercing his heart. The man let out a shriek as blood spit forth from his mouth in a huge stream. *"Fuck you, you piece of shit,"* the man said through the blood. Then he fell over and burped once and was dead.

The third Assassin didn't waste any time. He had a crossbow that he pulled out on the king. *"Here's to your bloody taxes, ya bastard,"* he sneered.

The arrow broke the air.

It moved silently, though, in that second, the King had slid three sharpened stars out from his waistband and thrown them with such ferocity that the warrior's ear looked to have just fallen off. The second dart went deep into his face, and the third, into his brain. His eyes rolled back in his head and stayed there, looking straight up. Cross-eyed, he fell forward. The weight from the man's body pushed the dart even further into his brain. When he hit the ground, he hiccupped once, then tried to take another breath, then toppled onto his side.

The King was covered with blood, surrounded by chaos, and he began to scream.

"AHHH," his mighty roar went out. Everyone close enough to hear cowered in fear. It was so loud; it was like time stood still for a moment; blood being sprayed through the air. The ground turned to mud and that smoke with a strange scent that attached itself to all, was everywhere. Then the king looked over and noticed me.

I was filled with dread.

That's all I needed now, this lunatic murdering me. Would the Archon still adore him? I started to make the *Sign of Solomon* when suddenly I became very cold and then hot all of a sudden. I saw a torrent spring to manifest about and could hear the whining and popping as the vortex came for me.

Lightning flashed and I rode it once again. *'How many times can I take this?'* I thought.

5

When I re manifested, I was in the corner of a darkened room. I could hear an acoustic guitar being played a bit off down the corridor.

Standing up, I closed my eyes so they could grow accustomed to the dark.

A moment later, I opened them and I could see much better. It was night and I seemed to be in a sort of closet. Noticing some of the things that occupied the room with me: some towels and a small table. Implements for writing and a few pages of recently cut stretched skin, I'm assuming lamb.

"Keep it down," a woman's voice ordered. Looking in, I saw three women laying on a bed together.

The girl to the left and the girl to the right of the one in the center, all giggling in harmony.

I looked out from between the rear of the ripple fold curtain of the valance. The light from the lamps shined through, casting the room in an eerie shade from the border on the curtain, being fishnet in design.

They all looked so delighted in each other's company. The girls varied in appearance and even though all their nightgowns were exquisite, the most regale was the one that was in between the two others. Her brunette locks gingerly bounced to and fro. The other girl's hair was of gold and the third was of an alizarin Crimson. In the corner opposite myself, I noticed two baroque style four-poster beds. Both perfectly matching in appearance.

Hearing a loud bang, then footsteps, the girls all let out a squeal. *"He's come,"* the three said in harmony with each other. Then, the two maidens scurried away to their own beds and laid down as if they were sleeping, and it was not a moment too soon.

There were three slow, consecutive knocks on the door, and a moment later, I heard her small voice say, "Yes, who goes there?"

Another second after, *"It is your King, my soon-to-be Queen. May I enter?"*

"You may."

He peeked in his head. Slowly walking in, he shut and fastened the lock behind himself. As he was coming into the room, I searched for somewhere to take a piss. Looking around, I found a planter and a vase, both containing flowers. I reasoned that they would be happier together. So I put all the roses into one and emptied my contents into the other.

Moments later, looking in, I noticed a bird: or a huge crow or some such flying beast, across the hall. However, as soon as I had thought about wings, my *Archon* manifested before me.

Straining my eyes in the gloom, there seemed to be an alcove across the way to the other side opposite myself. There was a counter where one could see over, to gaining a better view. I hissed to get the Archons' attention, one of her eyes glowing in answer to my call. It was the kind of glow that results from taking a drag off a cigarette.

Her top lids were heavy, they shone with that preternatural quality like that of a living gothic statue would possess.

Looking over, I noticed the maids were laying with their heads on their pillows now, though each had one eye open, making a witness to this late-night encounter.

The King and soon-to-be Queen was now laying in each other's embrace. Each a world apart, though bound by time and in the moment. I also noticed the Angel was fuming. Well, sort of. It was so dark you will have to forgive my vague sketch of the proceedings.

All of a sudden, I was aware that it smelled of Cinnamon and Opium?

"Sweets?" the king asked in a way to get her attention.

"Yes, my king," she responded.

"Will you do that thing you do?" he asked in a stuttering voice.

She appeared to be thinking for a moment, keeping him waiting, then said," Yes, my king." Getting out from beneath the covers she crawled out of bed. Finding the direct gaze of the maids and facing away from him, she dropped her nightdress, revealing herself. Noticing one, then the other maid's eyes opening. She wanted to laugh though, kept these imperial voyeurisms to herself. She slowly turned around and sank to the ground like a puma, crawling up onto the giant four-poster bed on hands and knees.

Pulling the heavy blanket back that was over the King, she put her hair in a ponytail. Her pear-shaped breasts barely bounced as they passionately kissed. Then, all I saw was her head bobbing up and down The Archon looked livid. Eyes now glowing. Since she was so close in proximity, I needed not to worry about being discovered.

The King was now making audible sounds that were disgusting to my taste though, the soon-to-be Queen was ravishing to behold.

She leaned up and crawled on top of him. I looked back over at the Angel. She appeared as if her wings had soaked up some of the darkness of the room and they began to flutter at an unbelievable rate. Her ceremonial robes were a bit open in the front, exposing the underside and the hint of the barely perceptible breast beneath. Her skin seemed to glow as she began levitating halfway up the wall and it seemed from my view, she was looking through it. Gazing beyond, into them. She wanted to be *inside* the Queen though, I assumed not in the same way.

Hearing the Queen moan a little, then getting up, she turned around and went to her previous position only reversed, facing the sleeping maids. Her perky breasts bent back, and the king just looked at her like she was a goddess.

The two maidens hungrily took in the sight. Both looked into their mistress's eyes and in return, she was gazing into theirs. The Angel was watching what they were doing intently, her long legs halfway open. Her hand just inside her garments, wings beating behind her, pushing slightly so she was barely hovering, against the back wall.

"Oh, God." The Kings insistent peak of enthusiasm declared. She just kept bouncing up and down, then a couple of more thrusts, considerably slower.

Next, the soon-to-be Queen got up and turned back around, semen dripping out of her little crack. I noticed my Angel was in ecstasy.

Suddenly, it felt like something was crawling up my back. Brushing it away, I investigated the corner just to make sure there weren't any spiders or some such creature there. That reminded me of the old man from behind the *Opera House*.

Then, it felt like someone grabbed me that was unmistakably a human. When it happened, I reached out to steady myself and grabbed a picture that hung on the wall.

I was braced, but in so doing was now supporting the painting that I could barely hold up at this odd angle.

Time stood still and nothing happened.

I could still hear the guitar down the corridor. *"Help, her!"* came a scream into my ear, and it seemed my brain, so with that, I fell into the table behind me.

As I crashed to the ground with a loud bang, I saw the ghost of a man in front of me. Enveloped in that white-hot and cool blue, signaling I was to be taken. His face was a distortion to behold and I grabbed at him, catching only air, for I only got a handful of the stuff that shades are made of.

6

Tesla coils ripped and popped as I was re manifested.

Once I had arrived at my destination, I closed my eyes to adjust my vision to the gloom quicker. Upon opening them, I quickly realized I was in a mine of some kind.

The King was there, though he wasn't fighting. All presently in attendance was a handful of those same Knights from earlier at the battle. Only now being covered with beards and a bit thinner as well. Some had their shirts off and another few were crawling out of a tunnel they had been working in. A moment later and two more appeared. Pix and axes setting up against the walls, lanterns were everywhere, hung from posts of their own. It was so incredibly congested in here I was thinking and then the worst happened.

"Ah, ah," doing everything in my power to not sneeze. "Ah," it was over and soon passed. I superstitiously made the Ashur Star of ZxTxS, over my head and chest.

There were two fully dressed Knights approaching the tunnel now. As they appeared, one of the clothed champions began giving the first one a hand out of the gigantic hole. A short second later and both were out, panting and covered in dirt and sweat.

The helper knight asked, "Is it *true*?"

"Huh?"

The knight continued, "*You* have- found *it*?"

The King put his hand on the knight's shoulder and looked him directly in the eyes and said, "Yes." Pushing home his point and so much more. The helper returned the King's smile with a look of satisfaction himself.

"And the disks?"

"Keep it down," said the king as he looked straight at me. However, I didn't get a chance to think of being discovered, for as I turned away from the *King of Prides'* line of sight, I found myself shielding my eyes from yet another lightning bolt. Igniting all my being.

7

I was so tired. So, incredibly, tired.

Walking, though, mud. So hard to pull my feet out.

Then, I realized I was sleepwalking and feeling like I was running from something. Though, when I looked at the route I had been taking, no one was there.

Going for a couple of heavier steps when suddenly out of the corner of my eye I saw a stand of trees and there was also a stream. How long had I passed out? I could remember sitting and waiting for the Angel and eating that strange fruit.

It was mid-afternoon. Presently, I had to find somewhere to relieve myself. Then, going down the slope and as soon as I reached the bottom of the glade, I jogged to the tree line and once inside, I found a place.

As I was finishing, out of nowhere I heard some heavy beast that seemed to be coming right for me. Gently sliding into the bushes, the hooves were at the full climax and abruptly stopped.

I could just make out voices. Peeking around the corner; it was two of the *Satyrs*. I could smell the *woods* on them and *piss*. The clouds overhead had a slight grey tint to them. The two animals were conversing with each other in a strange tongue that was foreign to me. The beings were startling to behold to someone not accustomed to such things. Their preternatural movements were different altogether from that which I was used to.

My reverie being broken, the two began to bicker. The brother opposite myself violently slapped the other. Once, then twice. Extremely hard.

The sound cracked through the glade. The victim started to pant and cry. The slapper began to speak in that strange tongue again. It almost had the choppiness of German, though it was completely alien to me.

After this interrogation continued for another moment and the victim pulled out from his fur a very sloppy made bracelet. The diamonds that were on it gleamed in the light of day. On one of the evergreens just next to me, a shade was there, *had*, been here the whole time. Though, I didn't think it was paying attention to me. It almost appeared as though heat escapes from rocks in the desert.

The victim thief handed over the bracelet. The punisher grabbed him by the face with a clawed hand and said some more torments in that evil tongue, his brother squealing under the pressure.

Then, another sound. This one, of hooves as well. The victims' legs started to beat back and forth. The other one looked frightened as well. When the sound was too unbearable to take and the ground was shaking as the sky cracked open, threatening storms broke with a loud crash.

The two Satyrs began to whimper with their tails between their legs and hands over their ears to drown out the dampening noise.

It stopped.

The only sounds that could be heard were their quiet sobs and the birds giving the garden entreaties of the day. The two Satyrs were braced for impact. Then, when nothing happened, they slowly began to look around.

Next, a curious set of circumstances played out when a young deer, this one was of the normal variety that I was used to seeing on Ha-Aretz, suddenly appeared. I had supposed that on instinct these average kinds of faun would be afraid at the sight of such creatures as these two other beasts.

Both males, locking eyes with the female. Abruptly the newcomer looked away, smelling the fresh dew on the bushes. Her demeanor showed that she did not fear them.

Then, almost faster than my eye or brain could grasp they were both on her. The weaker one broke her back it seemed in half and the leader of the two had her throat locked tight. The first moment I don't think that she quite understood the gravity of the situation, and a moment later, she was violently trying to escape. She was held taught in death's embrace.

The shade that was haunting my present vicinity seemed to grow erratic, sending weird translucent prismaphorms onto the dew and in turn, throwing gaseous algorithmic codes cascading all through the shadows.

Then, very quietly a woman appeared. She was wrapped in a gown of mourning with a veil of despair over her face. The robe she had about herself was translucent. Her body was a pale tone with an olive hue mixed in from the reflections of the grass. The way she held herself reminded me of those Greek goddesses from the stories. Her face was cast down and looked the complete picture of a melancholy *Olympian.* Strangely, she reminded me of my Angel. It was her gait that in they seemed to share similarities of some kind. I wondered as to her nature, if she had *Ichor* or *Naga,*' blood, running through her veins. That being the fundamental difference, between *Celestial* and *Qulophian*, though technically, I've never beheld one of the latter.

She looked up and the scene must have been horrific. The two Satyrs just looked dumbstruck. Blood smeared in the hues of killing across their male human faces. Pointed ears. Goats' beards. Shirtless. The natural splendor of depravity. Though, at the same time, it was also the nature of things here, spreading its clawed wings across the savage garden.

In a very calm voice, still looking down she said, "May I ask a question, Satyr?" Quietly, and meekly as could be done in this place. They both just gazed at each other and then back. Blood and fur fell in huge chunks from the younger brethren's faces.

Both siblings were as perplexed by her as the small deer had been of them. Either they didn't know whom she was talking to or they simply couldn't understand her words. Though, it didn't matter. Had one or the other had the semblance to speak they wouldn't have had time to utter a curse.

Another woman appeared; her eyes cast down as well. Then, out of the conifer closest to me appeared a third. The second one started to hum some tune that sounded remarkably familiar.

The little faun hit the ground.

"Blunk!" She seemed to be looking right at me. Everyone in attendance's gaze fell to the small broken animal.

Birds started to sing their song once again and it smelled like honeysuckle in the air. Then their attention was drawn to the first sister, "Excuse me, I asked you a question."

"Huh?"

"Do you not know your kind are forbidden in these parts of the Gan?"

"Uh?" he answered. The birds continued to sing.

"Do you not heed the words that have been deemed by our most high ancient of ancients?" The second sister asked from behind, more abrasive than the first. The weaker of the two Satires began to shake from terror. The first Goat started moving his head back and forth and pointing an accusing finger at his brother. Then, in turn, the first one began to shake his head, pointing back at him.

As the bigger Satyr was about to say something, his words were cut short, barely getting a little out in that language that is native to them. She cut him off. "Do you not know what you have done?" Then the two other Sisters closest to them in unison said, *"Thou hast surely spilled blood of an innocent."*

The first Satyr turned and ran. Though the second sister dematerialized and reappeared on the other side of the yard, effectively blocking his way. The Witch closest to the weak brother said, "Sister, show them thy promise."

"Yes, sister." The second Witch said as she slowly opened her robes, exposing her full breasts and hairless vagina. Both Satires, true to their nature, just slurred and were momentarily mesmerized.

"Yes," she encouraged. "Look."

Next, the first sister grabbed the weak brother and very roughly asked, "Do you and your brother want to see our other sister's delights?" As she said this she gently rubbed her lips over his.

Both goat men shook their heads. *"Yes."* Then, each Witch looked at the silent melancholy shorter of the three and said, "sister, show them."

"Very well."

There was a moment of silence as she dropped her robe, exposing the pale delicate back of her person to me.

The rain gently started once again. The rapture was mixed with blood and gore that ran down the satire's skin and fur. The rain fell in big drops that soon threatened to completely wet the nude Witch's long brown hair. This third sister reached behind her to where I could see that there appeared a dagger, picking up the rays of sunlight.

She knelt in front of the faun. It was still alive but barely. It was very calm, so the sister gently put a relieving hand on her shoulder. "I will be as merciful as possible to the innocent," she said incredibly low in a somber tone, almost a whisper. The faun violently tried to get up. After giving it a moment, she plunged the knife to the hilt, under its ribs, and into its heart. Its life stayed with it a beat or two more, its body fell limp suddenly.

Thunder cracked as the third sister screamed, *"I will be vengeance."*

"And I will be justice," said the second.

As the first Witch had the weak satire in her embrace, she seductively said, *"I shall be wrath,* and then bent back her head exposing two sharp *vampires' teeth.* Then everything happened extremely fast. I could smell a sickening stench as the macabre scene unfolded.

Letting out a fearsome scream, she bit the taller Satyrs' bottom lip completely off. Simultaneously, the second brother, watching the drama unfold, let out a cry at the sight of his siblings' lip being disfigured. Turning, she pulled out a dagger of her own. It had a star on the hilt with a crescent -shaped ornament adorning each side. She stabbed him in the back, *1,2,3,4,5* times. Her hand and arm moved at an unnatural speed.

As she did so, she let out a scream.

The sister that had appeared to me first was making some sort of incantation. Her arms raised, she began to levitate, appearing, to be talking in tongues. The rain began to slow, then altogether stopped. The shade was no longer visible and the smell in the air became one of *Abramelin's oil.* Then the witch's body completely lifted about a foot off the ground higher than before. A dust storm of the smallest degree began making a den of the leaves, sending them up and out to spiral back down.

The two unoccupied Witches were finishing off both murderer goats. Eventually, it ended with them decapitating each in a bloodlust frenzy.

The third Witch, upon finishing her invocations, was once again on the grass. Retrieving her gown and adorning it, she joined the other *Daemons*. They began speaking in low-pitched tongues albeit I gathered, that *The Furies,* were off to bathe. Furthermore, they just left.

Once I knew they were far enough away for me to escape detection, I ran as fast as I could in the opposite direction.

Chapter VI
Were all a little crazy, aren't we?

1

On a cloudy day in April 1869, the 300-man *Saint Louis County insane asylum* opened its doors to the world. Admitting on its very first day 127 patients that were transferred by wagon train from a very overcrowded state hospital in *Fulton*. Another eighty were brought in from the county farm.

The asylum was the second in *Missouri's* history. The first being Fulton State itself. It was the dominating psychiatric hospital west of the *Mississippi* albeit taking a lot of hard work from not only locals but those further abroad as well. For the first couple of decades, all pleas for the institution to be built fell upon deaf ears. It took the suicide of Missouri's seventh governor, *Thomas Reynolds,* in 1844 to get the enabling legislation passed for the construction of such an establishment.

During the erection of the vast building, bricks were made on-site and the crew worked six days a week. Shortly thereafter, a shadow was cast over the project when a suspension beam was somehow appended, causing the death of two brothers that were employed from the local area.

Then, during construction, on the second floor, one of the crew was at work digging at the well, when another chance circumstantial event occurred. As workers drilled, to their surprise, they discovered an exceedingly high grade of coal.

Procuring it took a full year of drilling first before they could cash in. Though, nevertheless, with the proceeds the family *Bliss* hurried their project to completion.

After acquiring the *coke*, the family kept and sold what was on the property's lot and auctioned off a substantial amount of the rest of the neighboring land as well.

Mr. and *Miss Bliss*, taking on the overseeing duties themselves, had a few weeks before opening been found dead. The usually happily seen couple had chosen a *lover's suicide*. No one ever came forward with any information, it was sudden, to say the least. Miss Bliss's mother and father, *The Robertsons*, quickly stepped in and took control of the estate and the deceased young couple's baby boy. Though, once the youngest Bliss himself grew of age, he took, '*ownership*,' of the family business.

The succeeding generations on the Bliss' property went well. The hospital on the other hand, sustained decades of escapes and an entire ward dedicated to the evilest crimes being committed by those who couldn't find a home upon release.

The crimes that went on behind closed doors there were considered sometimes far worse in comparison to the ones done '*outside*,' that had put the criminals there in the first place.

After several lawsuits, the family business was brought down to a single manor. The other parts were sold off as attorney fees grew. Now, just a three-story mansion is all that was to show. However, things had been looking up for the last *Score* or *Till*. The latest offspring was stretching his talons now, urgently signing a waiver to take in a female patient who was found wandering the streets early this morning.

St. Louis is no place to just be strolling around anywhere at any given time. Some cities are more akin to violent jungles than the pleasant suburbs and condominiums of the colleges of Anyville. The patient was found in the downtown district, mumbling about a demon or something. That it was taking her breath away. Well, when the owner of the café found her in just shorts and a T-shirt, he politely asked her if she was lost, and she kept on mumbling. Then, slumping down onto her knees, she started to cry. At this time, the owner of the café's wife came out and tried to comfort her.

"What's wrong sweetie?" The baker woman asked.

"He's *lost*."

"Who is lost?"

"*The Artist,*" she whispered.

"What Artist?" she warmly asked.

"The one who is *lost*. He's trying to find the woman."

"What do you mean girl, what *woman*?"

"The woman of suffering." Not understanding, she just looked down. Then Asking, "Bill, what do you make of it?"

"I don't know Jess. We'll ask Terry when he gets here and see what he says."

"Yeah, that sounds good. After we see what he says, we will just have her ride with Pat, to the E.R." Two early morning patrons were reported to have gone into the diner at that point. That's when she went violently mad. The two men had to restrain her until authorities arrived. She didn't provide them with any information. Though, once she was detained at the local police station, they tried to communicate with her albeit this just enraging her until they let her be. The nurse on staff gave her a sedative. Then they called Mr. Bliss to see if he could help. He told them to bring her on over, and they dropped her off fully sedated.

They were just now returning to their squad car. "Give us a call if you need us!" said the deputy that had brought her over.

"Sure thing," said The Doctor. His short-sleeved button-up collar shirt and mustache and glasses with his big curly hair cut quite the figure. He gently sipped on the remains of his small coffee, out of the small straw, from the small Styrofoam cup that he held.

Presently a security guard came walking up. "There he is,"

"Afternoon Doctor Bliss. New patient?" The man's mustaches would have rivaled that of *Frederick Niche.*

"Hey, Brady."

"Yeah?"

"We have another chosen to be blessed and made whole again, yes."

"Very good," the security guard smiled.

"You don't work until tonight, everything ok?"

"Hell yeah my man, it's payday. Just come in to grab my check," he said with a smile and started to walk away through the double doors.

"Brady?"

"Yo?"

"It's a full moon tonight, you know what that means?"

"Yep. Whole lota' crazy out."

"And in," the Doctor joked, and they both laughed as Brady went inside.

Immediately following his exit, the doors swung open as two male orderlies appeared. Both were around the same age though, one was slightly taller than the other. The shorter of the two wore a more serious look on his face as his friend being much more lighthearted.

"Hey," the orderly said.

The Doctor gave no introduction, just instructions as usual. "Take the new patient up to Nurse Margaret for a medical."

"Ok Doctor," the taller one whose name tag said 'Mike,' absentmindedly went about as he unhooked the lock on the wheel with his boot.

"What's up?"

"What did you say?" The Doctor asked from under his breath, his complete demeanor changing.

"Nothing. I don't, think?" Mike questioned himself. He and his coworker had smoked some *Shiva* on their way in today. Sometimes it caused him to make better decisions, claimed his dealer.

"Not you, you idiot," he said looking directly at him. "*You* Ernie," The Doctor said turning his attention to the other orderly. "You're going to stop talking shit," he said sternly.

'You don't think I hear you, whispering. You think your so tuff."

"Yeah, what are you going to do old man?" Ernie said, stepping away from the hospital bed. Mike just stood there watching it all.

The Doctor immediately met his standing advance. There they stood face to face sizing each other up. "You wanna know what I'll do? *I will fuck you up,"* he said. Ernie did nothing. "*I will beat your fucking ass,"* his tone growing louder with each word. *"I will dog walk you boy."* An old woman and it looked like a caretaker had wandered up. Their gazes never moved. *"How can you be so disrespectful?"* The Doctor asked.

"Huh? *Me*" said Ernie. *"You, are the one going off on me."*

The older man started to walk away and then stopped. "You're going to quit talking shit under your breath," he said simply.

"I didn't."

"But you *did*. And you *do*." It was silent besides a nurse calling for a *'one p.m.'* "I mean, you don't want. Hold on, let me start again. How's *Richard*?"

"No, no, no," Ernie said shaking his head.

"No. *Yes*," he began shaking his head up and down. "Yes. How is your father?"

"No, no, no. He said that if I get in trouble again this year-," he stopped. That same nurse was calling, *"two, thirteen."*

"What?" Ernie asked.

"*What*, did he say *he* would *do*?"

"Send me to the camps," Ernie said, with fear in his voice.

"Send you to the camps," The Doctor mocked.

The back door swung open, and he recognized the man.

"Father VenzVoss," The Doctor said. "I'll be over momentarily."

"I don't care. Where's The Nurse?" The big holy man asked. Looking back to Ernie thoughtfully. He said. "That is all. You may go."

"Yes Sir," Ernie said.

2

The patient silently breathes from under a mask. Her deep brown hair looked black in these shadows. "Mike, will you grab that door?" the shorter of the two hospital aids ordered, more than asked.

"Of course," the faculty gates snapped open. As they walked down the first gallery and through to the first-floor landing, the room was noticeably colder. Just as Mike was mentioning this, two different magazines were lifted, and tossed into the sidewall, seemingly of their own accord. The taller orderly saw, shocked, and stopped.

"Ernie, did you see *that*?"

"See *what*?"

"Nothing, never mind," continuing once again and a secretary pulled the little window to the side. Looking out, all that was visible was a clock on the back partition and blond bangs.

"Olson! Kinston!" She called. *"Is there a Stuart Olson or an Amberley Kinston out there?"*

"No," said Ernie. *"Mike?"* As he said it he nodded to the opposite door. Mike followed the request. They opened the adjacent door from the office, which led to a dead end.

Turning around, they quickly went toward the cafeteria. As soon as they came around the bend the lights in the main public area started to blink on and off.

"This place has always given me the creeps," Mike admitted.

"Oh yeah," said Ernie in a mocking reply.

The next door they walked past, the light would flash on and off, then back on. Staying off for a second and then the doors slammed shut, —effectively sealing this floor off from the rest of the wing on both sides.

They were trapped.

The light flickered but didn't go off completely. From the look at that end, there was the light from a closet on. The door must have been blocked or something because Mike and Ernie hadn't noticed it before.

Mike looked to Ernie for directions, and when none was forthcoming and Ernie feeling ignorant, he barked, *"well, I don't fucking know."* Then, towards the way that they were headed they stopped. Ernie appeared to be listening very closely, hearing what sounded like an entire staff filling a lobby. Then, out of the darkness came the long shadows and through that, came two children.

The boy looked to be a couple of years younger than his sister. As the kids approached the doors to this wing from the far elevator side.

"Hey," yelled Ernie to the children. They just stopped and looked down at him. The girl glared at the boy seriously.

The older sibling began giggling, which sent the other into a laughing fit as well. Each child, grabbing a handle of the door, swung inward. Thus, effectively closing the two men inside from this side as well.

"Hey," they cried as the doors were slammed shut.

"Bam!"

The light from the fluorescents flickered one more time. When it blinked back on, revealing the floor to be bathed in a greenish-blue light. It almost looked like a different room altogether. Gloomy appearing, like the humid summer dusks of youth. The doors along the gallery started to shake violently. It seemed as if all the occupants were trying to get them to open albeit couldn't for the doorknobs weren't turning. The strangest thing was, the man at the end of the gallery floor that just appeared as if from a fog that was even now filling the hall.

Ernie's first thought was that one of the patients had escaped. The man was at the door that they had come through from the cafeteria.

Head down. Dirty chin-length hair that was greasy. The only sound was that of the lights overhead and this person's strange accompanying hum.

The two orderlies looked at each other perplexed.

Ernie, being the one further away from the end of the hall, started to sweat.

"Run," said a voice in his ear. Mike heard it as well, for he started to panic and made his way around the gurney. The man, with head down, slightly looked up malevolently. Eyes still cast down too far beyond to see their expression. He began to slowly walk, still humming that old familiar song, getting louder with each step he took. The room smelled like mothballs and mold.

Then a curious thing happened. A poltergeist was seemingly turning over chairs and dropping paintings off the walls in an attempt to try and thwart off his advance. For one fleeting moment it did seem to stop him. A glowing sphere manifested before him. The Intruder spoke a few words that were too low to hear and soon the light faded away. The attendants were at the doors furthest away. The only thing separating them from him was the gurney.

The bed began rolling itself and the fluorescent lights started to blink on and off. The demon approached the sleeping woman.

As he reached out to grab the unconscious patient, there was pandemonium.

The doors leading to the elevators started to violently shake. Just on the other side of the frightened custodians, the lights blinked off and then on again and everything was close to how it was just moments before.

Same white fluorescence. Same background hum. The hall was in disarray.

"Boom!" The door cracked open. Mike and Ernie were never in their life this happy to see two police officers. Just behind them was a nurse and an elderly woman, all headed by Doctor Murry Bliss. Everyone looked undeniably surprised by the state of the place, except for Murry, who even inside wore his aviators. These were a dark yellow and you could barely see his eyes. However, one would not have to see them to be able to tell that he was furious.

"Gentleman," Murry said. Lowered voice rising to ten, *"what the hell happened in here?"* The two workers just looked at each other dumbfounded and back to *The Overseer.*

Then, a completely foreign sound shattered the silence.

"AHHH." The scream came from the figure sitting up on the bed. Straps loosened hanging at the sides.

The patient was awake. Everyone just stared at her. The only one who hadn't cried out was Murry and The Nurse.

Meredith had awoken.

3

"Name?" asked the nurse.

"I'm?" she stammered. Then the nurse rolled around on her stool.

"Miss?" the older woman said with her antique uniform on. The hat and sleeves of her shirt had matching red crosses on the arms as well. She wore a dress and sneakers.

The office the two women currently occupied was very discerning in the fact that the lights gave off a bedimmed illumination: bathing everything in that same uniform dingy green. This just adding to the general look and feel of the place.

The Nurse just looked at her, waiting. On the desk in front of her was an old clipboard and an ink pen clumsily taped to a string, which bound the two together. The smell of chemicals was strong here. There were framed degrees on the walls and some old pictures of the hospital itself.

"Look, if you don't cooperate Mam, you go back in the straps," said the nurse, with all the condensation of a woman with many bitter years of pessimism behind her. Both of their eyes found the straps on the sides of the doctor's office bed, then back into each other's.

"Meredith," she said touching the skin of her forehead. The Nurse took a careful observation.

"Don't you worry, we will give you something to fix you right up? What's your last name dear?"

"Hook."

Suddenly, it all came back to her. The violator grabbing her in her sleep. She felt vomit in the back of her throat. "I think I'm going to be sick," she said. Upon finishing the sentence, she began to dry heave.

She was supposed to be at work today. Anxiety, falling like an anvil. The nurse was bringing her a trash can.

"How long have I been here?" All the events up until the intruder came in were foggy.

"Two days," the nurse answered matter of factly. Then asked, "Age?"

Meredith answered the questions as best as she could. As she did so, she began staring out of the pair of windows on her right. They were heavily barred.

Next, out of the corner of her peripheral vision, on the back of the wall in front of the nurse, she saw one of the picture frames tilt.

Turning her head, trying to understand, she noticed the shadows growing longer or just that one frame bent from the distribution of its weight.

"Miss?" The Nurse asked. Only half concerned. Meredith started to sink into a trance. *"Miss?"* Something was moving along the top of the picture frame, throwing the balance off its hook.

A maggot plopped onto the far side of the desk.

Then another one fell.

"Plop!"

And another.

"Yes, um, does this hospital have a problem with bugs?" she asked in a daze.

"Well, no, I do the cleaning in this part of the wing. Here take this." Then dramatically, the nurse turned around to see what the patient was talking about after handing her a small white pill and a bottle of water.

"Take it."

She did. Then, saw the strange look on the woman's face in the reflection of the glass from the frames. She was staring straight at the back wall.

Nothing.

The pictures frame was straight once again.

Meredith gazed down and closed her eyes. The nurse just peered at her with that condescending look. What was going on she wondered?

'Ok! Ok,' Meredith thought. *'I've just got to get my bearings.'*

It's just she was feeling just so… Just so… Just so…

Tired, and her mind was a bit *fuzzy*. She tried to make sense of it all. Returning her gaze to the window there now appeared out from the tree, *squirrels.*

No, they weren't squirrels.

It was two cats fighting over something.

A bird's nest. Feathers were stuck in between the feline's paws. Then, as they were getting to the last of the meal, they started to play tug of war with the gristle parts.

"Did you hear me ma'am?" asked the nurse.

"No, my apologies. What I meant was,"- she had a mental break and forgot what she was talking about.

She searched for it. Starting to giggle to herself she almost remembered then, nope, it was gone.

"I like your sneakers," she lied to change the subject.

"Well, thank you," replied the nurse with zero enthusiasm.

"What happened? How did I get here?" she asked dazedly.

"Well, you showed up in a police car. By ambulance, from two sweet law enforcement officers," the nurse smiled with a detached look. Holding the pose, then going blank again.

"So, I was in jail?" Meredith asked. More to herself than to this lady. It was just now that Meredith noticed the nurse's name tag. It was above her left breast. The name looked to be scratched out, somewhere in time.

She focused her attention on it.

"Ma'am?" the nurse asked for the third time. *"Are you even listening?"* Her name was faded. To Meredith, the name on the tag started with an M.

Marker.

Margaret.

"Margaret," Meredith said. "Your name is Margaret?" she asked.

"Why yes," said the nurse. Her eyes bugged out of her head like a human-sized fly, adding to the malevolence of the gothic tapestry. All this she took in with despondent curiosity.

"That's a pretty name," she said, looking down a bit bashfully.

The older woman clapped her hands violently together.

"Clapp!"

Retaining that iniquitousness of the moment albeit bringing Meredith to full attention.

"Listen here, you little bitch," she screamed in her face as she reached out toward Meredith with a hairpin, tight in her fist.

Then the scene rewound several frames and the enraged nurse stopped. The film rewound and was back a moment before.

"Did you?" asked Meredith. Listening intently, only getting the low machine drone that was part of the background soundtrack to this place.

It was as if everything had stopped. Next, very faint, though not loud enough for the nurse to hear.

"Return."

"Return," she also said to herself.

The nurse was facing the opposite way, writing at the desk. Meredith could hear a machine beeping down the hall. Followed by some voices.

She said, "it's nurse Margaret."

"Run!" Screamed a terrifying sounding male voice. Meredith gulped and flinched. The nurse noticed her jerk her body back. Nearly hitting the wall.

Today was so… What was today, Meredith thought? The scene in front of her jumped one more time. Now, Margaret was looking at her seductively. "Why do you say that?" she asked.

"What?"

"Why did you ask me if my name was Margaret?" the nurse asked.

The noise out in the wing was growing louder. Then, they were directly outside the door and they all laughed at something. The humanness of it brought Meredith back down to Earth a bit.

"It was my grandmother's name."

"Oh, well, that's nice," the nurse said, and for a moment just stared directly past Meredith. Then she noticed another one of those big maggots. She cringed.

The nurse looked directly into her face. "You are a strange girl. You need to get a better way about yourself," the older woman said with zero enthusiasm and condensation, once again. Meredith shrank back as this exchange and was becoming instead of terrifying, something else.

Another maggot fell.

"Plop!"

This time the nurse turned, and then the door busted open. The sound of beeping machines and a full staff at rush hour followed. It was almost deafening. Also, a certain smell that she couldn't quite name but knew well.

The figure at the door was, how would she describe him? Basic. No. Eccentric. Kind of.

'He was a dork,' Meredith thought. As he was talking to The Nurse, it was hard to tell what he was looking at, his dark glasses shielded the observer from what was underneath.

"Not at all Doctor," the nurse said without making eye contact.

"Very good." He took a long drink out of his Styrofoam cup. "Bring the patient to my office after medical is complete," he said all this without even looking away once.

"-But doctor, we don't..."

"What? We don't, what?"

"Take patience directly back."

"Why? Because we don't know if she will *hurt me?"* He said loudly. His voice booming off the walls. He put his hand out for the clipboard. After a moment of contemplation, Nurse Margaret, gazed down at the ground in indecision, and relinquished the clipboard.

Meredith just looked on at this dance of *egos* they were playing. He looked at it a moment, then set it down.

Next, he leaned down to look closely at the desk, and with his bare hand, he slid his hand across it, effectively squishing one of the maggots off the table. Its body just fell apart from the impact. Its guts were a small disgusting mess.

Strolling across the antique room he appeared to be pondering the irony of it all, when he gazed out the window to the tree.

Turning, it almost looked like, he was brushing some lint off the nurse's shoulder.

Meredith didn't know for sure, but she could have sworn that the Dr. had indirectly wiped the remains of the larvae on the nurse. She seemed to not have noticed.

"Bring the patient to my office after your medical please." Though, it was not a question. He was looking down the whole time, as did the other woman. Almost, as if for a fleeting moment, they were lifeless.

Strange, she thought.

The doctor exited the room. The nurse got up and listened to her heartbeat. The stethoscope was cold on Meredith's chest, for the nurse made her take her shirt and bra off. She smelled like *Avon.*

Avon is what it was. Now that Meredith thought about it, it was more of a *stench.*

The nurse finished the exam after a few long moments and strolled back to her stool to the left corner of the room, and pushed a button twice. A moment later and two *male nurses* appeared. Well, that's what she thought their station was anyway.

"Gentleman," the nurse said. They stopped in their tracks.

"Yes, nurse Margaret?"

"Please transport patient Miss Hook to doctor Bliss's office. Then come back. I need you two to haul something off for me."

"Yes, Nurse Margaret."

"I'll see you Miss," The Nurse said. "As soon as the doctor gives you the evaluation. This evening, when you hear your name, go to the med window with everyone else. If not," as she put a wristband with her information onto her. "There will be consequences," she said and looked over at the two male workers. Nodding her head in Meredith's direction.

One of the men grabbed her a bit roughly under the arm. *"Come on,"* he said. She just got up and went with them.

Getting out of that room was a breath of fresh air. Immediately four staff members went running past. Their faces just lingered. In the next moment, she was hurried along faster. *"Look down,"* he said.

The taller male worker that was up until this point silent. He promptly grabbed under her other arm and hustled her along for about two minutes this way. She was ushered into an office and forcefully sat down, and then the men promptly left.

Meredith was going to call after them but her voice was lost. The sound of a buzzing fish tank stole her attention. She turned then, the scene in front of her started to unfold and her focus fell to the wall with the oak bookcase that was adorned with complete collections of medical dictionaries and law manuals. Some degrees hung in their black frames. The center of the desk then unraveled itself.

The doctor was there finishing a rotation in his big leather desk chair. A few picture frames were facing away from her on the desk. Then, after staring at her for about a minute from behind his glasses that masked his expression, he spoke.

"So, what's your story?" he asked

She figured she would just explain everything. He looked like he could be a reasonable guy.

"Who are you exactly. I mean, I know you are the main guy around here, but your facility hasn't given me any information? Why are you holding me here?" she asked soberly.

"My name is Dr. Murry Bliss. I'm the *Overseer* of the asylum," he said. Then, when the silence was complete again, he continued, "I thought my nurse had given you, my message." Leaning back in his leather office chair it slightly squeaked under his bulk. "Well, I told her to let you know I would be in to interview you as soon as I was done with *afternoon treatments*." Still, complete blank stare but with those damn tinted glasses on there was no way of defining his expression. Just blank.

"Treatments?"

"Oh, yes," and he stood up. "Do you know, *Miss Letter* is it?" he asked two questions in a row.

"Hook! Meredith Word Hook!"

He cut her off mid-sentence. "My ancestors put the first cornerstone upon the property. It was my great, great, Grandfather Bliss that got, well, all *this*," he said, waving his arms around the room. As if to take it all in.

This time she cut him off. "If you don't let me make a phone call, so *help me. I will shut this fucking place down."* Her intensity rising.

"Well, how are you going to do that miss Hook?" Crossing his arms with a grim dominance.

"I'm an attorney. I know my rights," she looked around the room a bit more judgmentally. Wearing a look of disgust as she clearly scrutinized a puma fur rug beneath a vast bookshelf that dominated the opposite corner. An Egyptian sarcophagus on the other side. Voices could barely be heard, more like a quiet commotion. Both their attention was pulled in that direction as the den became louder. The Doctor stood up. The fish tank bubbled.

As he was moving toward the door a book fell from the shelf behind his desk. Then another was slid out and promptly fell off.

They both turned. The sound got louder outside the door and another book fell. This time from the bookshelf opposite. He looked back and pointed at her. *"You be still,"* he hissed.

She put her hands up as if resigned. He went to the door and closed it behind himself.

There was a portrait that hung from an ornately carved gilded frame. The monogram at the bottom said it was a distant *Bliss* family member. Oh, so this must have been the creator of this place. As she wondered about these things; a pen rolled from her clipboard with a file next to it.

The pen rolled once, twice around, then commenced to plummet off. As it hit the ground the door opened. It was an orderly from The Nurses office.

"You got to come with us." They came into the room and just stood a couple of feet in front of her. She got up and the other man came in; all she saw was black. It was chaos. She was led out the door. They must have thrown some sort of bag over her head. She struggled just enough for them to note she didn't like it. As the trio rounded a corner the one on the right side said," trust me, lady, you are lucky you don't have to see this."

"Yeah, a real mess," said the other. They stopped.

"If you guys don't," her voice rose with each syllable. *"I swear I am going to..."*

There was an instant ringing in her ears that was followed by an unnatural silence. In this case, it was the confusion going on with the staff and what she assumed was the other patients. It was as if she were in a dream.

All of a sudden it was dead quiet.

Then, she realized that she still had the hoodwink over her head. She wondered how she knew the lights were changed before or the orderlies had marched her into a different part of the wing? Although she was rather good at retracing her steps, as soon as she pulled the hoodwink off her head, she was terrified.

This part of the floor that she had been led into was in a complete state of ruin and decay. The lights were yellow. The walls were a greenish color; reminding Meredith of something that would have been popular in the forties. The paint was blistered back in some areas, revealing black mold and the old drywall beneath.

The lights flickered on and off, extremely fast and then they did it one more time, for about ten seconds straight and all at once, it stopped. She dropped the hood unconsciously out of her hand.

Where had the two numbskulls gone? It all seems so much like a dream, but this was no dream, it was at best a nightmare. Meredith's head began to thump. She could feel her blood pressure around her ears pulsing. Directly in front of her was the corner of the hallway.

Carefully she looked around the bend. There was a long gallery with doors on the left and right. The first one up ahead was very ominous and sounded like someone was on the other side. There was a thick slap, that was strangely familiar. Chains were being dragged. She moved on from back the way she had come, hearing *'voices.'*

Was it The Doctor and his Nurse?

As she reached the second door of the hall, trying the nob, it was unlocked. The chatter and footsteps were getting louder. Her terror at being discovered was overwhelming. Just as they were coming around the corner, she slipped in through the second door. It was heavy and she closed it behind herself. As she turned around there was a spider morphed within a man's body, clumsily dropping off its web. An inner illumination glowing from within. Accompanying shadows, the dual ratios appeared as not so much as a dense inky substance that was dripping from tightly bound teats. Its legs had even more of the engorged breasts. Some were so swollen that they turned black. Others. Seeming, as curdled gall stones from where they had never been milked, turning spoiled and just rotting off.

It noticed her before she could see its face, coming upon her fast.

Once engaged, it easily wrapped itself around her like a boa constrictor. As she lost consciousness, she couldn't help but think the spider looked just like The Nurse…

4

Meredith awoke. She was being suffocated. Upon this realization, she remembered she was still in the hospital.

"OK. Stop fighting lady," one of the orderlies said. *"Be still."* They had started to strap her down.

The nurse came in, which caused Meredith to fight even more. The older woman stuck a syringe in her arm and once again the world became cloudy. She slipped into a peaceful sleep.

When she awoke, it was from the sound of beeping and low voices coming from out in the hall. She was loose from the straps, so she went and gazed out the window, needing to get out of here and back home but then again, she was so drowsy. Wondering out into the wing, she was surprised to find a single nurse on the island between rooms.

She could hear the television was on in the dayroom.

Going in and picking a seat in the front, she was just two away from the only other occupant of the room, a bewildered patient.

The lady resembled that of an old witch, with warm continence.

"Hello, *Meredith*," the crone said by way of greeting.

"What? How do you know my name?" Meredith asked drowsily.

"It says it on your name tag."

"Oh." Looking down Meredith saw her name, penned in ink on a sticker on her chest. The woman seemed to be paying more attention to the specter of someone else that was in the room, though there weren't any others present.

The lady said, "You shouldn't be here, should you?"

"It's a long story," Meredith replied.

"I think we have time. I'm Morda." After sitting down Meredith began to cry. She told Morda the whole story from start to finish. The only interference was when Morda looked around, replying ever so often to whatever apparition that was in communication. However, at the same time, her attention was all on what Meredith was relating to her.

"Do you think I'm crazy?" she asked. The medicine they had given her was wearing off.

"No honey. I'm just listening." As she was saying this one of the male orderlies came in and counted them then walked away. "I haven't had a real conversation in a long time." Then she fell off. She looked to be contemplating this last part.

"So, who exactly who were you talking to, besides me?" Meredith asked light-heartedly. To not upset the situation.

"The spirits. That's why I'm here. *I just can't get them out of, this place,*" she said tapping her temple. "You, see? This medicine they give us. Stops it... Stop them. *The evil ones from taking me."*

"You mean coming to take you?"

"Take possession of this body girl. To remove my soul and abuse my flesh." They set for a moment in silence as this sunk in.

The moment was only broken when the same orderly that came in a few moments prior appeared. "Morda, it's time for meds," she at once got up and went with the man.

"Hey, wait!" said Meredith. They both stopped and turned around. "Thank you for listening," as she said this Morda just smiled. Then the old woman looking off into the corner and started mumbling. The orderly impatiently guided her out of the room and down the hall.

Meredith stood there, happy to have a moment alone to gather her thoughts. Hearing voices, however, just as soon as they came, they were gone. She looked around cautiously. Her dark hair looked sculpted under this light. The two windows that were on each side of the TV were set back into a recess on both sides that looked over the front lawn.

There was a scent diffuser on one of the side tables. This room's wallpaper was the same green as the majority of the hospital's interior. It was this same hue that inspired the gloom that pervaded the current shadows.

The television, having only one nob to change the channels and two ancient-looking rabbits' ears stood like aged sentinels above the antique-looking device. After getting nothing but white noise and clicking from one channel to the next, she was gently shocked by the electricity from the static radiation.

Switching through the dozen or so options, she found that only three of the channels worked. After making her choice, she sat in the first chair, anxious to have her mind get away from reality for a bit.

She had thought it was a movie that she settled on albeit it was an infomercial about burial plots. The advertisement lasted about fifteen minutes and had many breaks for the commercials themselves within the program. She began to pass out, then shook her head a couple of times in hope of waking a bit. She remembered the nurse had said that she had been here for two days.

She shook her head awake again.

Now, on the television there was a very pretty lady that was dressed as an even prettier Angel. The whole time the infomercial kept its empathy and didn't lose any pride in the fact that it was a bit morbid.

She stood and changed the channel. The telecom was a live play and by the look of it it was *Hamlet*. She sat back down after stretching and yawning again.

There was the *King*, however, as soon as the smoke came and the weird sisters were there creeping about their cryptic business of prophecy, she began to think about the part when he gave himself up in a mental break. The fog remembered. For, it was the same as all the other condensation being completely recycled within *Ha-Aretz.*

Meredith's eyes closed, her head drooping. The shadows in the room grew in length toward her unconscious form.

She dreamt of angels and demons amidst burial plots.

Part Two
Curse to torment one, even in death

"Render thy circle impregnable."
-Aleister Crowley

Chapter V
Lessons of a different kind

1

Begrevra was known in some circles as a Daemon of the first class.

A *'Daemon,'* in this sense, *being a creature that had two natures,* or better yet, one with mixed blood from the two extremes of the *'Heliosphere.'* One good in a sense, and one bad in a sense. The reptilian side eventually would consume the other though, being the nature of the blood. A *'Daemon,' not to be confused with their closely resembling cousins, 'Demons,' of the first order.* On the opposite hemisphere from the *'Qulophian Demons' are their 'Celestial' counterparts, 'The Archons,' or 'Archonians.'* They are the watchers from above who inhabit the regulating *Northern Spheres of the Manx,* and for the last two thousand years have dominated to a minor or lesser degree on *'Ha-Aretz.'*

The ones who are on the knowing side of these revelations are deemed, *'The Demu,'* and the ones mindlessly blinded by ignorance, (this being the everyday bulk of the sheeple of 'Ha-Aretz,' who live better off in their *'Leave it to Beaver'* lives,) being known collectively as, *'Daywalkers.'* However, these are terms that are used interchangeably between, *'The Known realities,'* or their official title being, *'The Dementia.'*

Begrevras companion asked for a light. Handing the undead greaser, a zippo out of his suit pocket he said, "Keep it."

One who would describe *Barbados* as resembling a woodland hunter would describe *Begrevra as perverse destructionary.* Though, it would be hard to tell that from the looks of him. He seemed to get into some of the most, shall we say, compromising situations. Even now here he was, standing with two cold-blooded killers, waiting to talk to a retired *Magus*. Well, he supposed it could be worse.

Recently, while in the *'Mists of Ascension,'* a ritual for crossing through the *'Manx,'* Begrevra had strangled both of his spirit guides, causing such an uproar from the *monks of 'Havlla Monarchia,'* that they made it rain for a month straight.

That was not the worst part, and this is when it's hard to tell the rest of the story. You see, Begrevra, upon returning home, raped the mother of *Shtar*. Well, Shtar was his brother. Not only was this crime punishable by death among *'The Patriarchs of the Eternal Flame,'* it's looked down upon in all of *Ha-Aretz*, even by the most sadistic of standards.

Well, a few weeks ago, when father came home from the *'Legion,'* working for the *Militia*, he was not at all happy to find a new *Daemonic baby boy* filling his house with laughter and happiness. He promptly had it taken away to somewhere more fitting than the denizens of the *under spheres*. Begrevras brother, seeing all the proceedings, tried to intercede. Well, in so doing, got himself killed.

Begrevra, for his crime, is sent to *Ha Aretz: present-day Earth.*

It's said that for all his faults, he made up for them in dealmaking, or so the rumors go. He was the best Daemon for the job. His father *Oph*, needed this object that was claimed from one of the *Earth Tumuli.*

Seeing the opportunity to put Begrevra to work, he quickly sent his misguided firstborn to secure a deal to bring it through to his Sphere of Existence. Then, one day, he could destroy the link of Divine intervention and manifest his presence into the Celestial spheres, beyond the reach of the *Chosen Archons,* bypassing all the chaos shifts that come as a price for such feats.

Begrevra's thoughts were broken as the door was opened. There stood an older woman with long black hair pulled tight into a ponytail. "Hello?" She asked.

"Good afternoon, um, there," he said. "Um, my name is, Mr. Begrevra, and this is *Andres*." He nodded to one of the men behind him who looked to be from the nineteen fifties. "And this is *Ronove*." Seeing her surprised look at the men's questionable appearances, Begrevra nervously put his hand to his tie to make sure it was perfect. She looked over at his briefcase and raised an eyebrow. Setting it down to appear less intimidating, he looked over and smiled at her.

"It was a lovely day," the lady mused, looking into the distant west. All their attention was directed along her line of sight. The Sun was sinking lower and lower. "How was your day young man?" The woman asked.

"As well as um, can be expected, Mam." Thus, answering and not being able to hold back his true nature anymore, so as soon as she turned away Begrevras forked tongue flicked out, barely missing her face. Ethereally tasting her.

"Grandma," a human child ran up and latched onto the older woman's leg. Noticing the guests she hid behind her grandmother's dress, curiously eyeing the three new arrivals.

"We have an appointment," Begrevra said.

From the shadows within the foyer, they heard a man's voice talking to the woman. Giving her instructions Begrevra supposed.

"Yes," she listened albeit too low for the companions to hear from outside. "Yes, I will."

Meanwhile, Begrevra, getting down on his haunches as the little girl seemed to be mesmerized by his appearance. With a minor charm he produced a red rose. The little girl immediately smiled. He handed it to her.

Then Edna, waving her granddaughter away, looked the men up and down once again, then stepping aside, she granted them access. "Come in." They all shuffled in behind each other. Edna, peeking her head back out, looked in both directions and shut and locked the door.

She helped them put away their jackets and then led them into an anti-chamber to wait to meet with her husband.

As soon as Edna left the hallway, the bigger of the two henchmen went to the threshold and licked at the air audibly enough for the dead to hear.

Begrevra hissed.

A hallway ran through the length of the foyer they were currently in and there were two doors on each side. A huge painting hung on the wall, strange though, for all the guild upon the frame, the painting itself was left unfinished.

All three Demu approached it.

"Doesn't look like much to me," Ronove said from the right side of his master. The other man just looked at the underdrawing that was on the canvas, then down at the object in the figure's hand.

"Well, *he is,*" said Begrevra. "*Or was.* No one has seen him in the years since the death of his master *Ipso*. Father says he stays in communication with the *Architects* themselves so," and he trailed off.

"What's the big deal about this thing anyway?" asked Ronove, nodding to the disk. The child's laughter rang throughout the halls of the gigantic estate. Begrevra, being reminded of home, shuddered. "If it was meant to be known by all what it is used for, then you would surely already know what it is used for," Begrevra reasoned, then letting out another hiss.

One of the signs that the process was working its magic was the new habits he was attaining. Nodding to Andres, as if he were giving him the go-ahead, Andres threatened to smack the shit out of him though, he was just messing with him. Ronove flinched back almost hitting the wall. Begrevra and Andres both smiled but did not make a noise, letting Ronove let what just happened sink in.

Right then, the door on the other side of the chamber opened, seemingly of its own accord. Both henchmen just looked at their boss for guidance. After a few seconds Begrevra walked in, his henchmen following close behind.

The room was only half-lit from a fire that was going in the hearth. It smelled like sandalwood incense and sounds from the Opera House could be heard.

Magister Edward Hook stood next to an ornate bookcase searching for a volume. He had on a robe and glasses as he looked up with just his eyes as he regarded the three companions. Then, carefully scanning the back of a ledger. His long hair spilled in unkempt strands from the sides of his head. Upon entering, Begrevra very slowly said, *"Magister, is it truly you?"*

"It is," he said with his palms pointed up and towards the chairs that were in front of his elegant desk. Turning his hands over, flames began dancing off his knuckles, licking the air as they all watched.

Pyromancers, like the Magister here, were thought to have lost their gifts. One has not been documented for hundreds of years. They were hunted down by *inquisitors* during the *dark ages.* The *era* was dubbed *dark*, by the deeds of man during this era.

Paintings of neoclassical scenes dominated the walls.

After sitting, Begrevra opened his briefcase. Inside, there were many objects. Choosing a pen and notebook the other two guests sat there watching.

The small one just stared at Edward, and the other one looked to be staking the place out. Considering Begrevras bulk, he almost looked frightened of Edward.

Edward, flexing his hands, bones popping, answered, “yes?"

"Magister, first of all, um, it's such a very-" Begrevra searched for the words. “A pleasure to be um, in your presence," Ronove scoffed and Begrevra began to sweat.

The last dealmakers came back empty-handed twenty years prior. That was also a deal with the creator of the objects themselves, *Ipso*, but this was different. Begrevras father swore to hunt him down and consume him if the object was not secured. The first *Messenger* sent by *Oph*, in that case, mysteriously died two days later, due to a host of *'Ichalaris'* destroying his intestines and unknotting his colon, then unraveling themselves in a fit of orgasmic discharge that excreted, he shuddered to think of it, out of the sad fellows' piss hole.

It was a horrible sight. At this memory, Begrevra flinched."We have come to give you-," he stuttered.

"Come on," Edward prompted. *"What have you come for?"*

"I have come um, on my father's behalf, to give you the *password.*"

"Yes, *what is it*?"

"Silencium."

"Very well. We can discuss the object." They went through the rehearsed motions. "What deal did you have for me?"

2

Ronove was bored. Ever since he made his way to the other side he was requiring increasingly more and more of the strange magical substance of the ether, *'Oblivion.'* Even now, he was sitting there sweating and waiting on his next *particle ride.*

One day, Ronove reasoned, he would attain *'Ascension'* on his own. Then he would pervade through the Spheres and destroy all his enemies. Everyone who had ever crossed him. He would be unstoppable.

"Big dreams," his Pops would always say when Ronove would forget himself. *"Big dreams get you nowhere, except*

for anywhere fast. Dreams, yes dreams come true all the time, the bad ones. Big dreams and good things do not happen for people like us, boy. The quicker you find that out, the better off you will be," he would say.

The insults would progressively get worse throughout his father's nights of drinking. The last time he saw him, was after a particularly rotten beating when he went on a job with Ronoves uncle Billy. A few months later, Ronoves mother explained that there was an accident. His father, while doing a job, had gotten himself shocked to death from cutting into a power line. Billy 'the uncle,' had told his mother that during a long-awaited night together that he had done everything he could have done to help that day. The people from the neighborhood said that the corpse turned purple like a burned-up hotdog and his body smoked for hours.

Anyway, that was a long time ago.

Ronove was starting to get tired. It was from the endless watching of the password video repeatedly over the last two days on his *Tell*.

Two days journey just to get here, and for what? *The disc?* It didn't even seem worth it. Ronove was not exactly sure what the disk did, but he did overhear his two companions talking, saying that *Begrevras dad Oph*, wanted it so he could go to some forbidden place and challenge a guy he had never even met.

Seemed like a waste of time.

Ronove, also had trouble believing that this was the *Magister*, for the old prophecy told of the *Patriarchs* even before they showed up that day and changed his whole life. On that day, they looked so, so, much more different than this guy. It was the black robes they wore that was throwing him off. He looked at *The Magister* and tried to picture him with it on. Eh. Maybe.

Back home, with the *'Order of the Risen Slain,'* he had never met one of the Magisters in person. Though, knowing enough that to be a part of the *'Architects of Inception,'* the passion would have to be without blemish. Begrevra said, that just to be appropriated by one of the *'Legion of the Risen Slain,'* by the brotherhood, you had to do a minimum of five years' work, under an Adept of the Order. This, Magister Hook had worked under Ipso himself, which was crazy in the first place, considering all the successful conquests the older mage had led. That must have been how this guy had bypassed the brotherhood and went directly into Patriarch.

Once, hearing that Ipso was not even human and that he had *shadows* and *charms*, led one into believing he was. As he was talking to one of the *'Tzdilla'* back home, he asked it, why it was that that's what they were called.

It said that it was a title humans gave to any of the classes outside of their own sphere of sensation, and that he Ronove, was also one.

Now, sitting here wondering if they were even going to obtain the device today or not. His revelry was broken as they began.

"My father sent me to um, secure a deal so that in due course, he shall um, inherit the device."

"How is old Oph?" asked The Magister. When Begrevra just shook his shoulders, it was obvious they were not seeing eye to eye at the moment.

During the entire meeting thus far, The Magister, seemed to stair the whole time, *through* Begrevra, *into him,* Ronove thought, wondering if it was a challenge.

"What, may I ask, your father would do with such a device. Certainly not let it in the hands of, well, criminals like you, I am assuming?"

Ronove being clearly offended stood as if to say something. Edward just watched as the third man, Andres, guided him back down to his seat.

"You must excuse my guide, Magister," said Begrevra, as he looked back to Ronove. The word he silently mouthed to his companion was enough to make the henchmen's skin prickle from terror.

"Magister Two is my title. Magister Two, Tzdilla." At this, Begrevra flinched.

Then calmly, he invited his guest to continue, "you were saying?" Edward prompted.

"My father wants the device so that he may reach the sphere of existence, that is within reach of the," dropping his voice he clandestinely said, *"garden."* At this, Edward giggled.

"If I was prepared to make such a deal, what would be my end?"

"Um, your end? There is no end in sight. Except for the Gan,'" he said.

"Yeah, and this is how I know you're a *Tzdilla*."

"Huh?" This caught him off guard.

"My cut, for the object you idiot," Magister Two, said lightheartedly.

"Ten million dollars."

Slowly whistling, the Magister said, looking at Ronove the whole time with a sort of detachment, like he was there albeit somewhere else, "You know, when I was in my apprenticeship a messenger offered their services to my Master in exchange for the *Holy Touch.*

'After giving this man a chance, Ipso caught him stealing out of the coffers. We burned him alive and were the first ones to send someone through," the Magister leading Begrevra on into the rest of the story, holding out his hand so that the Tzdilla could finish.

"The Manx, via Trill, amid the Southern Spheres*."* Begrevra finished.

"And you have the talisman correct," the Magister silently shook his head yes. Also, Ronove ever so slightly breathed, *"talisman?"* Everyone in the room looked at him, he put his arms up to his sides, showing that he was innocent.

The Northern' and 'Southern Spheres,' were once thought fables. Forgotten about for centuries, being covered up and erased by Rome. However, only being suppressed to fuel their wars and fill their pockets at the same time. Then one day, evidence was secured in the form of the *'Video of Suffering'* created by *Magister One,* and his pupil, *Magister Two.*

As Begrevra wondered about these things, the adept conjured a flame right above his palm.

"Yes, we sent the camera through the Vortex," he said as the flame danced and licked the air once again from his knuckles.

"Yes, the *Vortex*," the daemon said, hypnotized to a degree.

"Well, Mr. Begrevra, as much as It was a pleasure-"

"Knock. Knock,"-and the door slightly opened. It was the mistress of the house, appearing with a tray of drinks. The scent of lavender followed her in.

At her sudden arrival, the room was filled like a breath of fresh air. That, teamed with the fact that everything had come to a dramatic interlude, was even better.

Giving the guests their drinks, she quickly set the tray down. Putting her hands flat on the desk, she steadied herself. Covering her mouth with her hand, she coughed a few times. Embarrassed, she apologized.

Begrevra, assuring her that no apology was necessary, was looking at her hand, shocked. Following his line of sight, she noticed what he was reacting to, she stammered.

Her hand was bloody and she quickly excused herself.

It was quiet for a moment, that's when Begrevra knew he had something to work with.

Looking over at the Magister he said, "I can give you more time with her." At this offer, The Magister became more interested.

3

A half-hour later and Edward was closing the door behind them. He looked out the window to make sure that they had left. The tallest of the two companions that were with Mr. Begrevra kept looking back at the house, taking it in, as if he were going to try to buy it, or burn it.

Edward hoped for the henchman's sake neither was the case. He began to go up the steps to his study when Edna came around the corner, looking at him dramatically for a moment, then they both burst into laughter.

After embracing each other, Edna checked that the front door was locked. The house, being strangely quiet since the guests left, their daughter came by and picked Meredith up so they were going to relax.

As he walked up the stairs to his study, he went over the deal he had just made. He had traded off the device. Not just yet, although, in return, he was to receive two more decades with his wife, and this creature held within its grasp, the power keep up such a bargain. The core of the exchange was, that upon Edward's *natural* death, in spirit, he would give up the object. Though when offered, he had only hesitated slightly, for the creatures would have to make enough sacrifices to appease his dark gods to even make the deal possible in the first place.

Thinking back to when he had first shown the device to one of his colleagues from *The St. Louis Medical University. James Hawks*, a physicist with a particular interest in fusion technology. Who in turn, led him on a journey to find its creator. A year later, he was standing at the front door of *Ipso* himself. However, he had to obtain blood by offering first, even if money has the power to call upon many malevolent spirits. The hardest lesson is from the sincerest, being the most *sincerely* haunted.

One of Magister One's first lessons.

Upon entering the compound, Edward quickly realized that the old adepti' already had an apprentice. However, in his old age, he did not so much care about the *laws of man* as much as he used to. He only bent under *universal law* now. The two of them hit it off from the get-go and after an evening in each other's company, Ipso decided to take Edward on. Over the next five years the mage revealed many strange things.

The grandfather clock chimed.

That was a long time ago. Before all the doctors. Long before even the Opera House came into his possession.

One of the first designs Ipso had given them lessons in, was to be able to fool people with shadows and charms, minor hypnotisms. Sort of like a mental sleight of hand. After these later shades were mastered, along with a couple of trips to a dirty bank in southern America, Edward was left with a small, but humble, fortune.

Upon his return from the *'Depths'* of his lessons, he met *Edna.* Next came *Claudia Rose*, who gave them, *Meredith.*

About a Till ago, Edna got sick and it has been getting steadily worse ever since. *"I do not know; everything should look up,"* Edward would say to his daughter Claudia Rose, trying to be as positive as he could.

After walking into his office, he made a call to the Opera House side of the property, to make sure all was well. With a promise to Monica to stop by that night, even if it was to make sure that the guests from earlier that evening didn't have the inclination to rob the place then he said, 'goodnight.'

All was well, for now, it seemed.

4

A few weeks after that, the intruders came in and messed the deal all up. Begrevra had no idea that one of his staff Ronove, was slaying prostitutes from right over the river. Unintentionally, he was drawing attention to the Demonic group that clandestinely operated within the sphere of Ha-Aretz.

Then, when local women's houses started getting broken into, that is when it got bad.

There were many murders. So many that the police, in their negligence of catching the criminal, began to tell the papers there were two killers, and they had caught the first one already, and that it was just a coincidence that the two cases were so closely related.

During Edward's interrogations and questioning of the trespasser, he found out many strange things. One of the details he had already surmised, was that the grievous father, *Oph Hashem,* wanted the disk so that with the proper names, one can create a *'Quickening,'* which the practitioners' sphere of existence is malleable. Then to take it a step further, adding *thaumaturgy*, which creates a *Maelstrom*. By manifesting a *Merkabah* one of them could traverse the *'Manx,'* without even needing *Ascension* abilities. In theory, across all the *Cosm* or *Heliospheres*. In all the *'Dementia*,' one would not be bound.

Now, here we are two months later and the deputy in charge of the unit informed Edna that the man who broke in, had been found dead in his cell, although his body was lost shortly thereafter.

"Ding! Dong!" The doorbell rang. He could barely hear it, for today it was especially loud, on the count of accommodation of the Opera House side.

Today was the opening day of a story about a deformed man, who after scaring everyone in town, jumps off the roof of his childhood home, plummeting to his death.

There was an irony to that.

As Edward questioned these things, he answered the front door.

"Mr. Hook," the woman asked.

"Yes?"

"We have your order from the hardware store. If you would just sign here, please?" She handed him an electronic block with a pen hooked to a cord. A strange device, Edward mused.

There was a lesson to be learned here as well, it seemed.

"Where do you want your order, Sir?"

"Inside. As private as possible."

"You did notice, Sir, that these bricks and mortar are for external brickwork?" Edward cut her off. He was so private he didn't even want to discuss it. He had to be careful because as soon as Begrevra and Ophs agents got wind of the situation, they would surely come sniffing around.

Inside, he invited them in to deliver the brick working materials. When they left, he gave them a generous tip to keep his business, his own. Oph was no joke. Edward remembered, that once he had sent a Messenger to Ha-Aretz to request an object from Ipso. Only after coming back empty-handed, did he poison him. Everyone thought The Magister One had executed the disorganization of the Daemons' guts. Nope, it was Oph. Ipso didn't care, "let them fear," he would say.

Edward worked for months, night and day on the corridor and rooms. As his wife spent long hours testing, to try to find out more about the mass. During these times Edward had to keep himself busy, had he not, well, he didn't want to think about that.

He manifested many *broods* to do the more arduous work in the moon-lit hours, then banishing them once they were done, each dawn.

He had a plan.

They broke their side of the agreement, so he would be damned if he kept his.

5

I came over the bend by the stand of trees once I got to the clearing. I just had to make it up past the weird monolith with the strange symbols on it. I knew my way back to The Angel's secluded garden.

It took around ten minutes to get there once I passed the glade of conifer. For all the anxiety that this place gave me, it sure was a nice day out albeit it seemed, like the terrors of the night was a distant memory.

As I rounded the top of the next hill the scent of honeysuckle enveloped me, I knew I was close, for the smell was tying together loose threads of experience. Then, I was startled when I heard an incredibly loud crack. The entire sky was dark for a moment, the stars even coming out and the bird's song had ceased. They must be thinking it's morning.

Then, as fast as the night came, it vanished. The birds went crazy, and you could hear the confusion in their song. It was an exceedingly bright day once again and there wasn't a cloud to be seen.

Way up in the sky, I saw what appeared to be a dragon. Like a giant serpent, it sailed among the clouds and got closer and closer overhead until I had to look away. It was too frightening. Setting my nerves to sunder, that even relating the events I'm wishing to not manifest such creatures.

A few moments later, it was like nothing had ever happened. The flying behemoth went in the direction of the twin trees from whence the lake came out.

Once again, I sat and began to feel overwhelmed. How long have I been gone now?

This place. This place seemed so magical, and I felt a connection with it, to a degree, for I have always been extremely interested in subjects such as these. Quickly, I realized myself once again and needed to find somewhere to piss. Then, going into the bushes up here by the courtyard, I found a hidden away spot.

When I was finished, I felt an incredible thirst. I remembered the strange fruit. First, I did a circuit around the Angel's small courtyard. She wasn't there, so I went over to the patch and looked through them. Immediately my mouth began to water. I selected one of the juiciest ones. They were that pale color, though, towards the bottom, they had a bruised hue about them that was the unmistakable nectar to be found within.

Just to make sure I didn't get surprised by a beating heart or something, I did as before and pricked it with my fingernail. Pulling a piece of the skin back and smelling at it, I found it was in all ways as it was before. A bloody tear escaped with the peeling of the skin. I couldn't resist and bit down into it.

It tasted just as it did before; actually, it tasted *better*. I gorged myself on the strange fruit. When I was done with the first one, I found its brother that was next to it, in the patch.

I decided that while I waited for the Angel to arrive, I would explore a bit. How much trouble could I get into up here?

I was contemplating the strange flying creature when I happened upon the other patch I had eaten from the last time. I instantly dropped the core from my second piece of fruit and went in search of the most bruised one that I could find, knowing that's where the sweetness was fermented.

Upon a detailed inspection, I noticed a big black slimy area. It looked as if some type of chemical had decimated two dozen or more of the exotic fruit. *'Damn,'* I thought. This patch, I will leave alone. I went back towards the courtyard.

I could hear birds start to sing their normal tune, signaling the afternoon was progressing into the evening. I was going back the way I had come and was going to grab another fruit when I gazed upon the patch from where I had picked it several moments prior.

It looked like a massacre. The two stalks had broken off, and it looked like they had bled to death or had their throat cut, which what had basically happened I realized. Red juice was everywhere, turning purple, though in some spots swollen and becoming dark in areas. Clots hanging here and there. Some of the others were already turning black with rot.

'What the fuck?' I said to myself. Then, looking down the rise, where the stand of trees was on the far end by the stream, was a woman. She was all by herself dancing in the suns patch. When she noticed me she started to wave me down.

"Hitha! Hitha!" she said as she tried to get my attention. She had on a pair of shorts and had exceedingly long hair. It was pulled back by two braids in the front, the rest spilling over her breasts, covering her nipples. I went down to the grass, past the monolith. As I approached the unnatural monument, my descent and momentum were only being abated by the gigantic sentinel.

"Holy shit!" The surface burned my hand. Not so bad though. I looked and made sure it wasn't going to blister or anything like that. Looking over I presently saw the woman come back into view between the bushes. She stood there and gave me a look of desire and appearing to be impatient, she went back to the left, just out of sight, hidden by the trees. I began to make my way down.

The birds picked up their song and the familiar smell of honeysuckle filled my head once again. The sky looked to be turning evening a little early, or it was possibly going to rain.

I entered the elms. Among the verdant bowers the woman was walking. There was a wall of green to my left. I followed her and a moment later I was standing in the middle of a glade surrounded by saplings.

She was gone!

This must be a trap of some kind I thought. Turning to go and there she was. Running full-on into her and we both fell. I said, *"Miss, my apologies."*

She said something soft that was unintelligible. She smelled so good.

My hand went out to her locks of hair. She grabbed me as I grabbed her breast.

We kissed.

Pulling me down to the ground she straddled me. We kissed again. She tasted so nice, mixed with wine.

Nice, with wine, was a good cocktail.

She leaned up, grabbing my hands and running them over her breasts. Leaning down we started to kiss again as she whispered something in my ear, I told her something back. A curious thing happened for, she started to kiss and lick all over my chin and face, she asked me a question.

"Ish arurah etz?" She said, or asked.

"Huh?" I questioned. She played like she was taking a bite from an apple. Oh, she was asking about the fruit. I shook my head "Yes," I answered, and that's when she changed.

"Sae Ish Arusha etz? Sae Ish?"

"The fruit," I said slowly. "Yes. It tasted incredibly good."

At that answer, she went mad, jumping off me and disappearing into the greenery once again. A moment later and she screamed from the clearing. Ok I thought, this lady is beginning to freak me out. I followed her voice and found her outside the stand of trees. When she saw me she began her litany once again.

Running up to her I said, "Hey, Hey, *Hey, Hey!"* My voice grew louder each time I said it.

Next, I tried to grab her by the arms but this only seemed to enrage her even further. Who knows what kind of brother, or father, or lover, she would alert. Turning around I found myself gazing into a familiar face.

Then realizing who it was, I ran into the gathering of conifers. I had been mistaken; it was no familiar face. The sister just began to giggle. Her vampires' teeth were terrifying. Just up ahead, was the clearing. If I could just make it to that I thought. Then another sister was in my way.

Turning around as before, this time instead of stopping I accidentally ran into the third Witch sibling. Unfortunately,

I slammed into her, almost knocking myself out. We both recoiled from the collision.

I got up and began to apologize. Jumping up unceremoniously she began asking me something in that same foreign tongue the girl had spoken in. It was something about that damn fruit. "Look, ladies." I had all their attention. "I was thirsty. So, I had one of the fruits. I'm sorry. I had no idea it was so precious to you." Then one of the Daemon Sisters started to smart off to me and the other ones stayed her, watching me.

Thunder cracked the sky. At the sound I was at once reminded of the satires. So, I began to wave my arms around in the Sign of Solomon to invoke powers of my own.

At this, the woman began to back away. Then, the smart ass one started with an attitude, and began mouthing off again. Her sister started getting irate as well. *"Look, ladies,* I didn't know if I have even done whatever it is, you think I've done." The first sister, while listening to the others, was fingering something just out of sight, it was a *dagger*. I *absentmindedly* just grabbed it out of her hand from behind her back, as she was listening to her sister dramatize. At once she began a fresh assault of curses directed toward me.

I ran.

I made it to the clearing, just to clumsily trip once again over a big rock and fell on my face. I skinned both of my hands trying to break my fall. At that moment the Archon appeared.

"Anineil," the Daemons said in a not-at-all good way.

She was there. Magnificent wings fully extended behind her with her eyes closed. The thunder had stopped. A tempest sprang around her that was kick-started by her wings, as they were pulled close to her body and then her eyes slowly started to open.

"Anineil," the sisters echoed to each other.

"Anineil, is that thou art's name?" I asked as the closest sisters repeated it. She was getting ready to spring in the attack.

"Anineil, that's your name, isn't it?"

"GO, Artist!"

Then, her whole figure elongated in a distortion of her face and she said, in that disquieted demonic voice that was many, *"Go!"*

I damn near pissed myself and ran, again.

A few moments later and I was pushed down when what appeared to be an explosion rocked the area. Then, two more collisions were accompanied by a woman crying out. I ran up and past the monolith, towards the courtyard of the fallen King.

6

Amid circle and symbol, letter and numeral, *The Messenger* sat cross-legged physically. *Mentally*, now, that was a bit more complicated. The mask he wore was for his protection, not the disciple with whom he was about to commune. He didn't want his image bouncing around the Heliosphere, upon an Echo without his visage being veiled. Some way.

'Working with the device did have its advantages,' he thought. Looking down at his crossed inner thighs. He saw where the flesh had finally started the process of *Transmutation.*

It had taken over eighteen months for the diamond patterns to even show noticeably, though now, over two years in, they were becoming more *serpentine* every day. This is a reaction of the mixing of the two types of blood, thus kicking off one's own evolution, into further reaches with the aid of *Operators milk.*

The room he occupied, could have been called vain to someone just laying eyes on it however, those of a different school of thought would believe it to be primitive or unimaginative.

For the messenger, it served its purpose. Looking at his watch, it was exactly time.

Now, he slowly picked up one of the stones and put it into the device. It gleamed blood red with little black speckles. The other two matching stones were sitting just inside the first ring of the circle, to the left and the right, thus completing the trinity, or *pyramidal halo.*

The moonlight coming through the window was illuminating the messengers' working area sufficiently. Anyone who could spot this stone would be hard-pressed to give up its plain location, for it came from a place that to speak of it would sound like madness, to recognize its name, would admit to the conspiracy.

The Messenger's *demigod* was pulsing for awareness. Being on the receiving end of the transmission he spoke the words of invocation.

All was silent. Two minutes later and the stone in the *phylactery* headpiece started to ever so slightly vibrate. The noise at the edges of the circle in the gloom alerted the Messenger that the other two stones were popping up and down. All three stones started to go wild magnetically and systematically.

Then, abruptly, they just stopped.

The beam connecting the *triangle of Art* suddenly appeared. The Messenger, squinting his eyes to the sudden laser lights that were glowing right it seemed, into his eyes. Even when he would close them, he would see a scintillating bluish-white.

Presently, the demigod of the *'Light Eternal,'* appeared. Glitching into the secondhand transmission.

The Messenger, opening his eyes and slightly hissing in the tone of Qulophian. "So be it," said The Messenger, short newly formed forked tongue licking at the air. Immediately a holographic image displayed in front of his reptilian-like vision. He opened his eyes -but barely, for in the dark, these images could be blinding. Seeing how one would have to be ready to receive such a vision.

"Cambria Adorn daemon," an older *Begrevra* said. His face grew into his full Daemon potential. His neck was pulled taut because to make these communications possible, one would have to have the necessary requirements fulfilled.

With head extended up and neck muscles pulled taught, his nose pulled in and amphibian-like now, Begrevras eyes were completely reptilian, despite the color being the strangest. For, he was only a *Transmute*, he would get close, but not like his father who had thick full-fledged Naga blood, running through him, as Ichor runs through the Archons.

"What is the situation," the virtual demonic presence of Begrevra said.

The messenger looked up and replied in a hissing voice, "Master, we have her. We are just, doing as instructed." Then taking a heavy breath continued, "We assure you, all will be prepared for the opening," he hissed.

"The blood?"

"We have it,"

"Kolada Ashton," the demigod said in form of goodbye.

In return, the messenger mocked. "Kolada Ashtum."

Then, as the messenger inhaled and exhaled, the demigod glitched out of his Sphere of Existence. A moment later and his lizard eyes blinked three times, long and slow. Quickly, they returned to normal, human-like, once again.

Now tonight, if all went according to plan, he and his companion would give the sacrifice Begrevra had asked for, and in return, he would bless the two companions with a *baptism*.

The only thing that was left now, was to prepare the candidate for the rite of passage.

Putting his glasses back on, he walked back into his office.

Chapter VI
Pale Moon Rising

1

Meredith was dreaming. Floating about the long hallway that was at her grandparents' house.

It seemed so long ago now. One thing she vividly remembers is how her grandfather always seemed to be about different tasks, preparing for something or another, it seemed. Wondering what he was up to, she gently swam through the air, gliding past masses of water and pockets of chemical spoors, just out of the way of noxious fumes from the mills and dumps. To try to figure all of this out she had to go back to that hall, only her mind took her back a little too far.

Clocking its pegs slowly to a stop, she came into consciousness.

She was waking up from a nap. Getting out of bed, she went to the door and called for her grandparents. When no voices were forthcoming, she listened close. This is how she could tell where they were at most times. There was a constant hum coming from the Opera House side of the building, feeling it vibrate the whole foundation to its core. Coming here so often though, she barely noticed it anymore. Going out into the hall, she thought it was curious when the bathroom light came on seemingly of its own accord. Next, she went to the older couple's bedroom and called for them.

Oh well, grandma must be down the hall, for she could hear her feet scuttle around back the other way though, when she went and looked, there was no one there.

Going to the top of the landing, the grandfather clock went off, giving her nerves a shake. Underneath it all, she could tell that something *'other,'* something extraordinary, was about. In that childlike awareness that only adolescence can perceive.

It was coming from the voices issuing from down the stairs.

Going over to the banister of the landing, she put her head through. Someone was talking to grandma, and grandpa wasn't there. Listening ever closer, she heard a male voice and went down to see who had come to visit.

Running down the steps, young Meredith was scooped up it seemed by a shadow, but it was only her grandmother's dress skirts catching her like a net.Then, hearing the man's unnaturally deep voice, she looked out from the sides of the fabric. Meredith was confused about what she saw, the face was blurry. Rubbing her eyes, she shook her head to try to get them to focus.

There were three of the men all together she saw. However, it was hard to tell what their faces exactly looked like, because the Sun was in her eyes.

The man talking seemed pleasant enough. His goatee was dark, she remembers that, and, he had an extreme sunburn on his face. Pondering it now that she is older, it very well could have been high blood pressure, or some such ailing condition to cause one's blood to boil over so. The suit the man wore was like a mirror, seemingly reflecting everything at once to her young mind, yet revealing nothing.

Bending down, he smiled and seemingly out of thin air, produced a single red rose. Holding it out for her to smell the scent, she smiled at its freshness and took it, marveling at the magic of it all.

The man waved goodbye, and her grandmother told her to go away with her hand, so she went to find her grandfather.

Running into the darkness, her pace was steadily reduced by a heavy cloud, so that when she came out a moment later, after holding her breath, she busted out of the other side. She began to doggy paddle, splashing around the curve of an hourglass that had a crack in it but she didn't know where from. The sand pushed her as if she were on a swing so that she was safely away from the sharp edges. She swirled around and around, as if being consumed by a black hole, into a distant memory that she might therefore soon forget. Her grandfather had his small charms and Razes about himself she remembered as she was delivered. Gently getting up off of the carpet, she looked about herself and smiled.

This particular time spot was from when Meredith she was around the same age. She can see it now, her running down that hall and grandmother looking so happy. Her hair was dark black back then, except for a few strands of grey that were pulled taught. She had those pointy eyebrows that were like arrows, that could command attention or rock away one's sadness into oblivion.

Grandfather was off to work on his secret passageway, which was just like the one from the side of the house, only this new one you could get through from the back. As soon as they would least expect it, he would jump out, giving Meredith and Grandma a fright as they would come around the corner. Also, remembering the skeleton keys that were for hidden drawers and cabinets, like the one in the wall that's upstairs, or the hidden one in the basement desk.

She tried to think back to any memories of anything that would give her a sense of *his* personality. There weren't too many besides the stories that he would tell her, she couldn't exactly remember any of them now though, sadly for it was so long ago, but these were the things that he did that she could try to draw a reasonable conclusion as to his general aesthetic. There was clearly more to him as a person on a deeper level. Time though, stood as a barrier between her and such revelations.

It was almost as if they were standing there in time, right next to each other, but the wall blocks their realization of one another's presence. A veil gently pulled itself over bloodshot eyes and tears, blotting stains upon the fabric, seeming to bleed what is spent.

The more she found out about her grandfather, the more questions would be raised. Even now, who were his dark friends who presented themselves that day?

Wondering again as to the feud between her mother Claudia Rose and grandfather.

It all being seemingly over by someone trying to break in and *unbeknownst at the time,* though finding out *later*, that grandfather had apparently questioned the intruder a bit roughly.

That's it.

All because he had burned a killer with a cigarette albeit in hopes of finding out why this *'Vampire Killer,'* had done it in the first place? To Meredith and many others, *Edward was a hero.* Though, nevertheless, being robbed of his moment, for the time must not have been right. Edward, as far as she knew, never spoke of the *incident*.

She resented her mother and didn't speak to her, nor her husband James anymore over it all.

To Claudia Rose, in her reality, things were just a bit different.

Trying to find the underlying cause of this, she supposed, it was all due to her mother being somewhat negative and her grandparents being on a more positive level. Even though, *she* Claudia Rose, acts all high and mighty, wasn't it *her* that was a promiscuous alcoholic back then? Ultimately, she surmised, that some people just held hate in their hearts for their own personal reasons. Maybe it was all due to expectations.

Then, letting it all go, she breathed, and a bubble came out. Laughing, it made her stomach feel like she had butterflies bound within.

Still in a dream, Meredith floated up and into the sky, right above the Opera House. There was a light tug on her astral cord from below, looking in that direction, she saw many people doing the same things as she was, sort of roaming about aimlessly, not really knowing what to do or where to go. At the same time, she felt a soft pull in many directions that was distracting. She stopped and surveyed the cord. No one seemed to be causing it any distress. In the time she was contemplating it, it had stopped.

Then, Meredith, awaking from her dream, slid a little out of the chair in the hospital day room.

"Huh?" she said as she came back to consciousness. The nurse was asking her something.

Her face looked blurry, almost demonic, taking on such qualities so as to appear to be glitching in and out of her frame of reference.

Rubbing her eyes, she heard footsteps walking away, and then the clear doors clicked shut, locking behind the night nurse.

She got up, yawning, and stretching. The disgusting dinner this evening had made her tired and the scent diffuser did nothing to rid the stench in the room. Hearing something around the corner by the doors, she went to investigate the sound.

Going into the bathroom and looking around both stalls were empty. She thought to herself, *'what if there was someone in here, and I couldn't get out for help because the doors were locked?'* She laughed. If only they could see me now, she reasoned, they would for sure think she was crazy.

Looking deeply at her blurry reflection in the mirror, she thought, *'what if, I am crazy and had a nervous breakdown?'* they would laugh at her and perceive her to be an idiot.

The *'they,'* in question, were her coworkers. They would jest that she would go mad from being alone all the time, they were probably right.

Thinking back to the couple of romantic relationships that she had ever had, well, there was not much of a story to tell you on that besides the two serious ones she *had* pursued, had ended in bitter failure and she figured maybe dating wasn't, *'for her.'*

Feeling like she was the proverbial *Black Swan* albeit she wasn't against letting the dark bird extend its wings for a night or two.

As she exited the bathroom, she heard the sound again from the day room. Turning, she looked back towards the hall, and nothing was there.

A figure stalked her from its negatively charged existence lurked.

Levitating. *Watching.*

It followed her out the door. Whips of smoke were sending smoke rings through the air.

Going back into the day room she again went over to the phone and picked it up. As before, it was dead.

That's when she saw it. It was a mouse. It had a small candy bar wrapper and it was carrying it around, seemingly trying to pull it through a small crack in the wall. Then, she saw something flash off to her left.

It was on the far side of the room.

Standing, she went over to the recessed window and saw that on the property next door, they must be having a party. Then realizing, that if a car pulled up at just the right angle, each time it would cause such a phenomenon to occur, headlights splashing like pale phantoms upon the wall, appearing as specters.

She went back over and turned the TV up a little bit louder. When she sat back down there was a cold draft that made her shiver and she put her legs up in the chair to get a bit more comfortable.

The manifestation levitated behind her, close to the wall.

After the commercial on the TV was over a movie came on. When it started showing the credits from the beginning, she liked the music and there was a violin playing.

It was amazing. Oh, it was a live version of the second act of *Spring* by *Antonio Vivaldi.* Resting her head on the wall for a moment, she started to feel drowsy and her eyes started to droop so she shook her head to wake herself up.

On the television, there was a street sign and a couple of convenience stores in the frame as a truck pulled up, and then away from a small café. A woman was limping along after the smoke from the exhaust had faded.

Sporting a black eye, the expression on her face was that of one who has thrown up and is questioning if it will happen again. After opening the door and hobbling in, she eventually made her way to the counter.

"Two packs of *scream*, Sir?" she asked the clerk.

"1850 Mam."

"Did you know that *possession is real?*"

"How many Mam?" the man asked.

"How many *what*?" She questioned.

"How many *possessions* are real Mam?"

"Well, I wouldn't begin to know."

"Well, seeing how it is you that had *brought it up,* then I would say, a couple. Though if you want to try to catch them, then that's where you go," the man said pointing across the store, back towards the doors.

The woman followed his gaze.

"But is it *safe*?" She asked.

"*No*, it's not safe. Stay inside. For, if you go out there you will break every bone in your body."

"Why would you say that to me?" Said the woman. Then she grabbed her screams and headed out the door.

"To try to save you a lot of trouble, *lady*," he said as the crowd went wild with applause.

Meredith heard a voice, almost just felt it. It was crystalline in structure; it was feeding off of the drips of the sad thorns of summer. The fragrance was from that place, that she could remember from just past her grasp. If she could only stick her hand through the crack in the hourglass, she could shatter it to see what's beyond.

"How do I get there?" The man stood up and went over to the doors of the store. Then, looking out between the stickers on the glass, he kept pointing.

"*There*, you, *see*?" He asked.

"I don't want to see," she replied, nervously messing with her hair to make sure it was right, then flinched back at the ache from her swollen eye. There must have been someone else in the store because the studio audience began to cheer as another guest came in and ushered the woman back into the truck. Smoke from the exhaust obscures the view.

That was such a long time ago now, it seemed.

Her head drooped.

The shade knew when the time was right to strike. As soon as Meredith fell back into the astral realm, it joined in her dreams.

The clouds were so soft, feeling kind of sticky, like cotton candy. Though, as soon as she willed herself to, she landed, softly on the grass.

Approaching the pavilion, she sat down on a park bench that was down the street from her house.

There was a woman in front of her, sitting at the picnic table. The sun was behind the figure so that they were silhouetted.

It turned around.

"Meredith. "It was Morda.

"Morda, can we finish talking now?" Meredith asked enthusiastically.

"Of course, what do you want to talk about sweetie?"

"The Artist. The one that I keep dreaming about. He's always painting. He gave grandfather the one canvas with the key, and he gave him the one of himself that hangs in the hall."

"I know, I know honey." Morda hugged her. "It'll be OK. Don't you be fretting on no artists right now; he'll be just fine." Then Morda nodded to the astral being that was just out of frame.

"I know what to do now," she said to it.

A tear fell out of one eye and the words on the page are blurred beyond recognition.

2

I made it to the garden.

Hearing more screams, I ran to the Archonians rock of mourning and waited.

That evening, when the sky began to change colors, she appeared. I began to speak as she approached but she quieted me. At that moment, she looked so human and beautiful to behold. We walked over to the massive stone together and she motioned for me to sit with her.

"The name that thou art has called me is true," she said. Her ceremonial robes were freshly bleached and colored. Her skin held a translucent hue and I perceived she was much older than she appeared, I couldn't say for sure.

I began to tell her that I knew it and that it was a beautiful name, but once again she stayed me in my discourse.

She touched my hand, and in so doing, revealed unto me a vision. For, as she was feeling my flesh, it was more like a shared experience, as opposed to forced, directly into the crown of my cortex as before.

Then, a mocking echo reverberated in my mind's temple. Correlations connecting here and there. Drawing conclusions upon itself. Every possibility that was ever imagined could be grasped and manipulated through this entity. I knew at that moment, that what existed in the echo was going through each perpetual motion, almost like a broken figure eight, controlling me and every other being that's bound by a soul within this existence, collectively known as the Heliosphere.

Her finger felt like it was lightly shocking me again. A film was beginning, three, two, one.

Like I had with, 'The Oreads,' I was watching the negative existence of it all unfold. A mighty gothic cathedral filled my mind, the dome of it, big enough that you could fit a small moon within. Inside, the vaulted ceilings were grand and dripped off the saviors and virgin goddesses' blood in which they were built. Adorned with cross and flail.

Next, that prideful king and his group of Templars found this, said object, that they have launched entire campaigns in search for. Entire generations were wiped out, cities destroyed as buildings were leveled, all in an attempt to chase and locate the object. Now, armed with the *'Sang Greal,' the King left the Holy Land,* though instead of taking it directly home, the *Council of Father VenzVoss,* decided to make a stop.

Upon its attainment they visited *Roma,* to get the acquisition appraised by *'The Bull.'*

They were brandished complete and *Holy Knights of the Reawakened Vision;* their entire future had thenceforth brought them great prestige and material wealth.

The King, becoming prideful, lost the favor of his beautiful queen. His campaign's being so long that the queen, in his absence, grew board of his prideful quests and slowly started to fade from him. This, infuriated the King, even further, igniting his own demise.

His insanity's growing increasingly intense with every waking hour. His days were full of hate and when he would stop to think, he would become enraged all over again and afterward, would break down. In his moments of despair, he was cruel. The whole time the Angel was falling deeper in love with him, not accustomed to such raw exposed feelings and abandon. She liked his vanity and the unflinching monster that escaped him from time to time. When another of her brethren saw the attraction of hers for the King, they quickly revealed this abstention to their lord.

Then, one day, the King, being especially fired up over a letter from his wife, went outside and beat a man for not meeting his direct gaze. His thirst for pain being unquenched and passing the jail, he saw an old comrade who related that the man standing by, having squires mount his steed, was a criminal of the worst kind, one of those who prey on the weak. Just the night before, as they were drinking in their cells, the man of the cloth, was to be bailed out the following day and was laughing and jesting about how he had done this several times over. The king not putting up with such things strangled the priest in front of a small congregation and several others. They all witnessed his bloodlust.

Then, realizing a little too late, that this man that he killed wasn't from the jail at all, he was there to administer and witness a dying criminal last right. Looking over in confusion at the comrade who had told him about this man in the first place, and he was gone.

"Kilma," the King yelled his name, but for some reason, he couldn't remember the man's face.

Ashamed and still angry, he withdrew to his quarters. Requesting a stop to the *'Oracle,'* a strange creature that was said to be a *'Torso,'* with several, *'operators.'*

The townspeople, on the way home said that its gifts of prophecy were without equal, even by those in *'Delphi,'* that had long ago lived oddly close to where that old Emperor was that they visited, 'The Bull,' of Vatican City. Although upon passing through, the details were scattered and they were not able to locate the entity at that time.

Later, fevered, and mad, he would attempt to use his ferocity to his advantage when he was at the front of the lines of battle. On that particularly bloody eve, he took on two brothers and got a long steel shoved clear through his gut.

The Angel saw, in his moment of death, that he was reaching for her, and to her surprise, he could see her.

When his life's blood started to escape him, he beheld her and reached out his hand and the whole of the situation, she knew that his sense of pride was so great, he was not to be accepted into the celestial halls.

The Angel rebelled and intervened in mortal affairs by avenging him. That day, her master gave her the name *Anineil*. Before being known as *'Isha.'*

For her crime of rebellion, the lesson for her feelings, to prove herself light again, must face the *'Ordeal of Suffering,"* to become the *twice-born and consecrated.*

'The Ordeal of Suffering,' is when, instead of *Erasion*, being self-explanatory, this *Baptism*, or *Ordeal* was one of the eternal flames. Said to be given to all in the Heliosphere, by the hand of, 'ZtxxtS,' himself.

In this case, burning on a stake for three human days or seventy-two hours, amidst heavenly spheres. Exaltation, and death, not being an option. For, her host, was a jealous one. Her master wanted her to gaze upon his shadow sphere and behold her mighty *True King* for she seems to have forgotten his face.

I saw a mad fury of Archangels with that same piteous expression.

Though, the guilt, the guilt was stronger than anything. The only way an Archonian could feel the urge to end it all is by that highest paternal guilt. That only a mother or father knows how to properly deliver.

Then, I saw her, *proud*. They stripped her and she burned. It was violent and mechanical and I won't relate more to what I had seen.

I felt anguish for her and wept. We sat in silence, both looking down at the ground in consternation and momentarily contemplated the dirt, from whence we shall return.

3

"Yes. I'll tell her," Morda answered the specter that was communicating with her—guiding her.

"Meredith, now I need you to listen to me. *Will you do that?"* Morda asked in a strong tone. *"Can you do something for me?"*

"Of course, I can," she said from her younger self.

"Sometimes people go through things sweetheart." Meredith laid in her embrace, and Morda allowed it, holding her all the tighter.

"When people go through these things, their realities can become confused."

"Why can't they just remember what path their on?"

"Point of reference dear. It just depends on where everyone is standing in line, and everyone being able to understand that they all have a place, just when the boat gets rocked, that's when all the problems begin.

'Some people, it's their chance to *live*," Morda said while giving her a tight hug. "And some people it's *not*."

"I don't want to die," she said.

"Don't worry, sweetie. Now, it's not your time. You're not going to die, but *sometimes*, people *do*," pausing to take in a deep breath. "Now remember, when you get a chance to shine, you do it. You need that light to shine Meredith. To light you through the *dark place."*

"What *dark place?"*

"The land of sacrifice. The land where the *feathered serpent and land of the winding snake meet."* Meredith looked confused so Morda backed up a pace. "These fits you've seen me have, in the hospital?"

"Yeah?"

"Well, these fits, that's, how do I say it, um. I'm open, to being possessed, by others, you see?"

"Yeah." It all started to make sense. Her distant gaze in the hospital, and her frequent outbursts. It did appear now, in retrospect, that she had been fighting an inner battle that whole time and it was all under the guise of mental illness.

Then, she saw Morda younger, in different situations. Always explain to the Doctors that: *'The Demons are trying to take me.'* She would scream and yell all day and night long, that the *'demons were inside of her,'* and she would scream and go hysterical. Here we are fifty years later.

"The medicine they give us, in the hospital block receptors, then inhibitors that close the path of my echo, that can be mimicked throughout the *Heliosphere* though, one of the medicines side effects is, that my echo cannot be obtained."

"Wait, what? Heliosphere? I have no idea what that is."

"It is from whence all relative consciousness, well, within our, yours and my, *Sphere of Existence* or that have ever even thought of witnessing, is bound to.

The Astral Medium that holds within its embrace the collected *Solar System,* that within beats the heart of every earthly soul that has ever lived within Ha-Aretz. The prime component is hydrogen."

"Ha-Aretz?"

"Earth, and Earthly ish *Dementia*, contained therein."

"I'm so lost," Meredith admitted. *"Astral, systems, Dementia, what is this all about? What's it has anything to do with me?"* She asked plainly.

"A lot sweetie, more than really matters to your point of reference right now, "she said as she patted her, showing affection. "Mostly it's about good and bad ideas Meredith. Now, *these, people are sicker and more demented than anything you thought before. But you got to fight until you have no more fight in you."* Morda's demeanor became frantic. *"Do you hear me?"*

"Yeah. Exactly what people?"

"Do you hear me?" Mordas words echoed through the Heliosphere. Then she looked startled.

Then extremely fast, and directly, she was physically, pulled away.

Immediately Meredith opened her eyes.

"Morda." She quickly got up and walked to the bathroom. At this angle, she could just see the clock and avoid the gaze of the night nurse on duty.

Nine O'clock PM.

They had a patient count every two hours at five after. The nurse was busy playing on her Tell, as Meredith smoothly snuck by. She walked past the rooms until she reached Mordas.

Entering the room, she saw Morda lying there in her bed, sleeping.

Meredith instantly felt a sense of relief, this is what happens when you wake up from an astral dream she supposed.

Walking over to wake her, she felt such a close bond with her now. Then, sitting on the side of the bed, gently touched her shoulder. Rolling her fully on her back, Mordas's blank eyes stared back at her, meeting her gaze, from the depths of her sunk-in sockets.

Meredith quickly put her ear to the woman's chest. She sat back and just let this sink in.

Reaching over, closing her eyes, Meredith felt that she was still warm. After checking her pulse, then she knew that she was surely dead.

Two tears automatically fell out of her eyes.

Then two more, hitting one of the drops of blood at the corner of Morda's mouth, which found the cracks on the wrinkles and went like a spider's web all through to her chin.

Looking down, Meredith saw the sacrificial dagger in her gut. Sobbing, she then remembered Mordas last words she had said. For her to fight back no matter what.

Then she was *angry*.

Chapter VII
The Patriarchs of the Eternal Flame

1

Edward was in the waiting room when he found out Edna had died during surgery.

He was devastated. He loved her so incredibly much. All their years together, the child they had done all that they could for and of the mornings sitting together, drinking coffee and eating cinnamon rolls. Just the warm feeling of being in each other's presence.

All of that's over now.

Ever since he moved on from his old life, with all that craziness with, *'The Order'* and all its insane *'Patriarchs,'* his life had dramatically changed, and for the *better*.

"Fuck it. Back to hell with it all," he said aloud. They could all get fucked. Let it all burn, *Andalusia, The Spheres, even all of Ha-Aretz, just not Edna.*

That was where his heart was and would forever, thou shall remain.

He went into the hospital room one last time to say goodbye. However, those dark moments, are not mine to tell.

2

"Goodbye father," Claudia rose said. "-and I just hung up."

As far as goodbyes go, she reasoned, it wasn't that bad. Hell, she had heard worse on some talk shows for sure.

"Well, that's to be determined," the therapist told Claudia. She was currently at a counseling session.

This was the result of one confusing night; after a few drinks, she had tried to claw her husband's eyes out. Well, he had to physically hold her down to get her to stop attacking him and in so doing, got punched in the face a couple of times. This drama unfolding gave rise to the neighbors being fed up because it had gone on for several hours, so they called the police.

He said it was as if she were possessed by a strength that was not her own. Well, in the process, *'James,'* her husband, had slapped her, defending himself, when she had backed him into a corner. It was a complete clusterfuck.

Then, when the authorities showed up, they called it a *'domestic,'* and had to take someone to jail. Claudia and James were handcuffed sitting on the front porch. Afterwards, arguing to the point of getting arrested because they simply could not keep their mouths shut.

Now, here Claudia was, explaining herself.

"And then what happened?" the therapist asked from behind her reading glasses—chewing gum without a care in the world.

"What?" Claudia asked. She seemed to be in a daze. It felt like it was a bit too bright in the room and the air was stagnant.

"What did you do about your father? I mean, all he wanted was to see his granddaughter."

"Oh, I never really thought about it like that." The counselor wrote something down. Then blew a bubble. Claudia continued, "does that count against me?"

"No, no, of course not," she scoffed. "Tell me again about what happened, the night before the incident, at your house recently."

"Nothing really, I just had that terrible dream. The one about the painting on dad's wall, that I have every now and again."

"Tell me about that. Actually, no," the therapist said, as she grabbed a set of notes that were next to a file on the desk.

Then, reading the first page," tell me about what happened when you were, um, just out of high school."

"Nothing really, I just got caught with some Booz."

"It says here, that yes, you did get caught with alcohol, underage, on more than one occasion," she said, raising one eyebrow above her glasses, blowing a bubble. Claudia flinched when it popped.

The therapist continued," and you were a runaway at the time, and it says quote, *"Claudia Rose Hook of St Louis Missouri charged Friday the twenty-fourth in vehicular manslaughter, found guilty. Receives time served, and two years' probation."*

The therapist whistled, "how did you manage that?" Looking over, she noticed Claudia was just glaring at her, tears welled up in her eyes, anger just beneath the surface but not quite to the boiling point yet.

"Look, these are issues that over the next few months, we must try to tackle, or I will not release you from your court-required anger management classes. So, the quicker you work with me, the faster we can both be done with it," she said soberly.

"I, don't, want, too," Claudia said slowly, anger rising just a cunthair.

"I, don't, give, a, shit, what you want or don't want. You don't get told *'No'* much, *do you*?" She said this without an attitude or anything but a clear restrain and a lacking tolerance for bullshit.

Shaking her head, the therapist began, "ok, well, I'll do the honors, Mam." She picked the notes back up and started to say something else and stopped. Taking off her glasses she rubbed the bridge of her nose, and after a pause, she asked, "after all the love, and money, that your parents invested in you, and put into getting you out of trouble, you just moved away and never let them see their granddaughter again. Says here, *one Edward W. Hook of St. Louis Missouri filed several times for rights to see Meredith that year, and then his lawyer followed up with more Inquiries, with no response.* Can I ask you something, Mrs. Williams?"

"I don't have to take this," Claudia said calmly.

"What did they do that was so bad, to make you abandon them," then she took a breath and finished," at the end of, your mother's life?"

"I don't have to take this," she repeated herself.

"Who's Meredith's father Claudia? *Who are you trying to hide?"*

"I get it, I fucked up and I can't help that now.

"You definitely got that right," the therapist agreed. Claudia started to sob again.

"It's listed here you don't know who the father is. *Who is the father?"*

"I don't remember," she said with tears streaming out of her eyes. *"If that's not good enough for you, I don't know what to tell you."* Standing, she started to grab her jacket.

"Walk out that door, and I'll make sure you never see that baby when you have it." Claudia just looked at the therapist, dumfounded.

"How did you?" she started to ask.

"How could I *not*," she said smartly.

Then they both just sat in silence. The tension in the air was thick enough to cut with a knife. Claudia, collecting herself, began, "look, I moved away after it happened, I met James. We got married, and Meredith grew up and moved to the city, end of the story," she said flatly.

The therapist, putting her glasses back on, grabbed the file and started leafing through the contents, looking over at Claudia a couple of times before asking, "ok, so, Meredith, tell me about your daughter."

"Nothing much, she is just like any other kid I suppose," Claudia said distantly.

"Actually, she really was a good kid and now a full-grown adult."

"You act like that's surprising."

"Not at all. I'm just being objective," she blew another bubble. She crossed her legs, high heel bobbing back and forth.

"What are you trying to prove? Is this all necessary?"

"That remains to be seen, Mrs. Williams," she said, taking off her glasses. She gazed over at the clock. Damn, only fifteen minutes had gone by. "Ok, let's back up some, what did you, *'like,'* about your parents?"

"I can tell what you're doing, and I don't appreciate it. You think that your so clever. Well, whatever you are trying to *assume*, that I didn't love my parents and that I was a shitty daughter or whatever, well, *you're wrong*. I did love them, and I do miss them. *It's just, it's just,"* and then she broke back down.

'Well, it seems like you got a part of it right,' the therapist thought to herself as she handed her a box of tissues. Claudia had to fight the urge not to rip them out of her hands and bash her fuckin face in, but she knew that would get her nowhere.

"Are we done yet?" She asked, looking over at the clock. It had been not even twenty minutes yet.

"Eh, we still have a few more basis to touch on, for this session." The therapist looked back over the file, seemingly reminded of a question. "What about Jessica Mars? What did she have to do with the accident that landed you in jail and this whole mess revolves around?" She asked looking up from her notes.

"Jessica, was, the accident," Claudia said nonchalantly.

"Oh, -and what happened?" She asked without looking up.

"That night, I was driving Jessy home, and um, a car, by the track sideswiped us, as we were making a turn and, we flipped. Jessy died," she said flatly. "I have done everything in my power,"-the therapist cut her off.

"You mean, you guys had been drinking and, just dropped off her boyfriend. Then you, Claudia, you sideswiped an elderly couple, killing everyone but yourself and you were luckily, just underage."

"I know, I messed up, but I have done everything in, I mean, everything I could have, and I have to live with that for the rest of my life. Knowing that I-," the therapist cut her off, dismissing Claudia's guilt.

"Ok, *did* you learn a lesson, because you basically got off with a slap on the wrist?"

"That's why I moved."

"Yes, that is true. Says May of that same year, you filed a restraining order on *Scott J. Mars.* Tell me about that."

Looking down at the napkin in her hands Claudia said, "Scott was her brother. He tried to kill me, after the *'accident,'* and all her friends tormented me, until I moved," she said honestly.

"Ok, and Meredith's father?"

"Look, I suppose it doesn't matter now that they're dead."

"What's that? "Asking what she meant.

"I had a *crush*, or, I mean, I was *in love*, with one of *dad's friends*, but he *forbade* it, *and I still hate him for it."*

"Why? He might have been *protecting you,* especially since you were *underage*."

"I *didn't* need *protecting*," she said. Again, looking down at the knotted-up paper towel.

"What was this man's *name*," she asked without looking up from her clipboard.

"I don't *remember*, "she said.

"You do."

"I don't," Claudia said flatly.

"Mrs. Williams, -."

"No, no. I don't think you understand. My father could *do things."*

"Such as?"

"Change things, I mean. Um, this is going to sound crazy but, *he made me forget."*

"Forget? *Forget what?"* The therapist asked.

"The man's name. He completely just, *wiped it out. Gone.* He said that he would make sure it was over, *and he did.*"

"Ok, ok. I think this has gone as far as it's going to today."

"Thank god," Claudia Rose said.

"Oh, so, what brought about this last incident? The dream that you had from the night before that could have been the underlying cause?" She asked.

"Yeah, so, in the dream, a guy, was facing away from the picture he was painting though, it wasn't a real painting. It was like some pages from a book, but it's the baby's dad's name, written in *blood.* So, from there I saw a shadow, that went by a map of Egypt. Next, I woke up, mad as hell. Then James started on me, and I snapped."

"Huh?"

"Strange right?" Claudia asked.

"Eh. Not too strange," the therapist said.

"Do you plan on seeing your daughter ever again?"

"Most likely."

"What about your husband, James Williams?"

"Nothing. That's it. He's my husband," she answered, looking down at her barely perceptible bump.

"One day, I'll remember his name, and then, he will come and find me."

"OK, well, Claudia. I'm going to write you a prescription for something that will suppress the nightmares."

"OK, that sounds good."

Claudia never had any more dreams of phantoms or demons, that were not her own. She just carried on in her own rotten existence, with visions tormenting her later down the road. They were of her old friend Jessica, pulling her down, under the still waters of a black placid lake.

3

The funeral for Edna was incredibly beautiful, though horribly ugly, in another sense. Edward almost felt like he didn't belong there, one group of women and a couple of their elderly husbands were sitting at the back by themselves, chatting it up.

Along the front row, on one side, sat Edward, and on the other, Claudia Rose. Knowing he would have this uncomfortable situation over with soon enough, Edward just sat there, in quiet contemplation.

Claudia on the other hand, was arguing with her husband, 'James,' with her Tell dinging every few moments. Each time it would go off the women at the back would quietly begin a new round of *Oos* and *Ahs.* Since Claudia wasn't adhering to the signs that said that once inside, all Tells were to be shut off.

Moments later, and the cycle began afresh. Then, a man in a suit came out and whispered something into Claudia's ear and she clearly shut it off in front of him. Edward thought he overheard something like, there was another service being conducted on the other side of the building and something about, *'respect.'*

Edward just smiled, he had been growing a bit, how shall we say, aggravated in his melancholy state.

Claudia, faced with one more visit with her father, didn't bring Meredith along.

Edward felt so alone.

That was the last time that he saw his daughter. It was one of many long black days. Shortly thereafter, he would try to phone, and nothing.

It wasn't long before Claudia just ceased communication with the old man altogether.

Then, a few months later, Claudia told Meredith that her grandfather had passed away and that he was with grandma now. These last few years Edward sank deeper and deeper within himself.

4

Meredith was sobbing.

She had found someone who she thought that she could look up to and now they were gone.

The door at the far end clicked open with a jerk and footsteps were getting closer and closer down the hall toward her. When they came around the corner, she noticed that it was one of the orderlies.

"Wow," Mike said. Stopping dead in his tracks. Meredith looked at him and sobbed.

"Well, I didn't do it, if that's what you're thinking," Mike shook his head slowly back and forth, showing her that he could tell. "I get it. What happened to her? I just brought her back from Meds no more than twenty minutes ago."

"I don't know. I had a crazy dream, so I came to check on her, and this is how I found her."

Then Ernie came in the heavy door and strolled around the corner, *"holy shit,"* he said as he walked up into the murder scene. *"What the fuck is going on in here?"* He asked. Then looking over, "oh, so the old bitch *finally croaked."* He acted cockier than Meredith cared for, so she jumped up and got in his face.

"You watch your fuckin' mouth," she said. At being told what to do, first Ernie was quiet. The buzz from the machines droning along. Then, he started to get aggravated. The whole time Mike stayed out of it, as he could see that Ernie was about to snap.

"What of it bitch?" Ernie asked, pushing out his chest. Meredith walked up to him.

"What? Are you *that mad?"*

"Yeah and?" He spoke. Spittle coming out of his mouth.

"Look man, we all need to get out of here," Meredith tried to explain.

"We, don't, have, to do, *shit,"* he said as he poked her in the chest.

"You keep your fuckin hands off me," she said and slapped him. It looked like it stung but Meredith was no match for a grown man. He slapped her right back.

"Hey man," Mike said. Then, as Ernie went back in to smack her again, he just ignored him. "Ernie, now listen to me." Then he went to hit her a third time and Mike tried to grab his hand.

He struggled, then turned around.

"What the fuck Mike?" he said and pushed him with both hands. "*You want some too?"* Ernie asked.

"Look man, you shouldn't be going and hitting girls," Mike stuttered.

"Look man, you shouldn't be hitting on girls." Ernie mocked. "I ain't never hit a girl that didn't *deserve it."* When he turned back around, Meredith was gone.

"And now where is she, *you fuck,"* he said to Mike. *"If my dad finds out about this,"* he squealed in anger. Leaning down on his haunches, "man, he is going to fuck me up for real this time. *Shit!"* Then, a dinner tray busted over his head.

"Boom!"

Almost losing consciousness, he shook his head to try to get his balance correct.

"Hit him," Meredith yelled at Mike.

In the confusion, he really didn't know what to do. Ernie howled in rage. Then, slipping in the soup from the tray they all stopped because they heard a bang. Like an image frozen. One, two, three times.

"Bang! Bang! Bang!" Then, Ernie tried to get his balance but as he started to get up Meredith picked up the tray to hit him again, but he grabbed her by the wrist, pulling her down. Slipping on the wet floor she fell on top of him.

"Stop it, both of you," Mike yelled. The banging began once again. They both got to their feet and Meredith started to slap at him furiously, letting out a fearsome roar. Ernie grabbed both of her wrists and punched her in the face,

falling onto Mordas gurney and in effect knocking it over with a loud bang.

Her body crashed to the ground, it rolled then crunched into the wall, blankets going everywhere.

"Ha," Ernie laughed as Meredith struggled to get up. He turned around to Mike, *"and you, stay out of this."* Then noticing Mike's look of alarm, he turned.

Meredith was standing there, sacrificial dagger tightly gripped in both hands.

She must have retrieved it when she was over the corpse. What made everything worse was that there was a banging in the background every few seconds, like a pulse-pounding metronome or a drumbeat of death.

"Stay back," she said. Ritual dagger pointed out. Ernie looked away, then he looked at Mike and said, *"Get her man!"*

"Boom!"

"What the fuck was that?" said Ernie to Mike as if he had all the answers.

"Hell, I don't know, Ernie, ease up, man." Mike tried to reason with him, but Ernie looked to Meredith.

"Maybe you would show me a thing or two?" Ernie said, licking his lips. He rushed towards her, and she screamed. Then, they were pounding on the glass doors. That must have been the drumming sound. It was a security officer accompanied by Dr. Bliss and Nurse Margaret.

They unlocked the doors and stomped in.

5

Brady didn't know what to do. Everything was happening so fast. Just a few minutes ago it seemed, he was just getting here for his night shift. Shit, he's only been a security guard for five months.

The crazy thing is, that when these types of situations happen, protocol says that he had to follow the Doctors lead.

Seven years on the force and a stray bullet in the leg put him here, basically a rent a cop. Now, here he was, next to Dr. Bliss and The Nurse, trying to talk down not a patient but one of the staff.

Ernie had wrestled the knife away from Meredith and put it to her throat.

"Hey," said Dr. Bliss, all pissed off.

Even The Nurse spoke up. *"You, Ernie. You, let her go!"*

Then Brady said, *"Boy! Now, you, let her go! There is no sense in dying today."*

"I don't even know how this happened so fast," Ernie said.

As soon as he let go, The Nurse and Dr. Bliss cried out, *"he's going to kill her."*

Ernie, in this overly excited state, launched to take Meredith hostage again and then Brady shot him. Hitting him in the throat with one bullet. Ernie, falling backward, hit the ground, his skull making a sickening crack on the tiled floor. Laying there with his eyes open, looking straight up as if he were going to say something but was cut off mid-sentence. He made a soft but wet choking sound, still looking up the whole time.

"Wait what?" Mike asked.

Brady, looking over at him, saw only a flash, and then all faded too red, to grey, to black.

6

"What the fuck?" Mike asked.

Smoke coming off the small barrel of the Doctors handgun, Brady collapsed, just to land awkwardly and still hold himself up. After a moment, he started to try to stand.

"Boom," and if the first bullet didn't do it, then the second one surely did.

Brady, still standing as if crouched upon the second shot, at once tilted his head back, looking directly at the nurse, and slumped back against the wall. Eyes staring at the nurse all the while, never leaving the spot again in this lifetime.

The silence was deafening suddenly. The steady, beep, beep, beep, and Mike had to look away. In so doing followed Brady's gaze. Hearing Meredith scream, he looked over and saw that The Nurse now held a syringe that had a strange glowing substance inside. The liquids thirsted to be out Mike thought as he saw a bit of the stuff dripping off the end of the needle tip.

"What the-," his voice was choked off as the nurse and Doctor just stood back. *"Fuck lady,"* he finished.

In a surreal moment, Mike felt at his neck. Instantly it began to itch, grabbing at it, it felt like a bee had stung him. Looking over to Meredith, she ran up and pulled the needle out of his neck and ran to stab the nurse with it.

"Stop right there-," Mike heard as he got lightheaded. Thinking he could stand this head rush out he collapsed ridiculously hard on the ground. As Mike lost consciousness, he thought about how he's allergic to bees and how if he gets stung by one, he could die from it.

7

It all happened so fast, and now Meredith was locked in a cell with the orderly, Mike.

He was passed out from something the nurse had given him. His neck was really swollen but hers was too. His bastard friend would like to have strangled her. Little help he would have been. The Doctor had killed the security guard too. Shot him right in the back of the head. That seemed like something a coward would do.

Next, he had overpowered her and dragged Mike down here afterward.

The Nurse made sure the doors were locked. Still wearing that weird blank stare, like she was looking through you, or a macabre caricature of her true nature.

That hidden one.

Meredith saw a strange mass play amidst the shadows and wondered if this was Morda's way of communicating. She just hated this waiting game more than the whole hospital and all its weird people and all the bullshit that came with it. This all made her feel so claustrophobic ever and anon this damn cell just made it worse.

Meredith went over to the barred windows and put her hands around them tightly. Gazing out, she noticed how brilliant the moon was tonight.

8

Under the same glowing Moon, though a different constellation of stars, Edward was looking out the window and thinking about what just happened.

He tried to call Claudia, but she had changed her number and moved. Even now, three months later and still no word or anything. Not even a *'fuck you.'* Edward made a phone call to one of his old acquaintances who could find out, *'certain information.'* She told Edward that his daughter probably didn't want to be found. This is when the neighbors would say that the lights were always on at all hours of the night and there were strange people and happenings there. This was when Edward had his last go-around with the *'Order,'* keeping the worst as far from his mind as possible. They say that he had a few various influences around his Sphere of Existence though, that's a tale for another day.

Then, the scene changed, and it showed Edward inside of a scientist's office, yet it kept the same baroque and rococo charm as would a fifteenth-century mausoleum for the holiest of bishops and priests alike. He and this other man were chatting and laughing it up when they strolled down a long hall with piping running the length of the ceiling.

Approaching the corner, as they took the turn there appeared a big machine or more appropriately, *'Particle Collider.'*

They were busying themselves with making observations when the scene changed yet again, and here both were discussing a ready-made magus circle.

The man was teaching a younger Edward, sitting cross-legged in his monk's robes, both of his apprentices close by, awaiting instruction.

"Are you ready Edward?" Ipso prompted, from his ancient-looking meditation pillow.

"Ready!"

"What about you?"

"I'm ready two," his female apprentice replied.

"Now, close your eyes." Both initiates did as their master had asked.

"Do you feel it moving you?"

"Yes," they both said. What Ipso meant by, *'Moving,'* was the waters and vapors spreading unto physical sensation after ingestion.

"OK," he said a moment later. *"Let's go,"* he added.

In that direction, both candidates opened their eyes to the astral realm. They found themselves levitating right above the compound.

He was by there, brilliantly illuminated. *"Come on,"* Ipso commanded. All at once, he swam through the ether into a chasm, in the ceiling. The two initiates followed in the older man's path in his sphere of existence.

"OK," Ipso said from his physical body. "Now remember the place to run if you get lost through the houses?"

"Yes," they both said at the same time. Dodging and weaving past the buildings in the neighborhood Ipso flew at an unfathomable speed with both his apprentices trailing just behind.

"Here, we, go," and they were pulled along. It seemed as if they were being yanked because they were up, and up, and up. It reminded Edward of the expansion of time. It seemed

as if they were as high as airplanes could even go but still, they went even higher than that.

Edward started to feel like it was hard for him to breathe when his female companion reassuringly put a soft hand on his chest, for this comforted him.

Then, everything was so fast that it was hard to tell *what* they went through.

A gel here that almost caught them up as all three of them barely missed some hydrogen isotopes. Edward then was almost held by a pocket of gelatinous matter.

Next, when it seemed like going higher was too hard, he bade them keep ongoing.

Finally catching up to Ipso, they all got into the shade of a big piece of steel from an artificial satellite. "Why do you always come up here?" she asked

"I come up here, to not feel the pull."

After much coaxing, the students had talked their master into bringing them. He told them they would be able to travel there as soon as they were ready. Well, two years in and this summer night was as good as any. As this was happening, Ipso was flying around like a seasoned expert.

"Shouldn't it do the opposite, you know?" she asked

"Well, you would think so," Edward spoke for him. In mind, Ipso explains the main reason thus, the sun is where our souls end up, well, those bound for such a destiny and the photons that are expelled, is so much information. It calls the spirits to be quiet, over mind; in turn, Ipso is blessed with a moment of silence.

She hugged Edward and marveled at Ipso. He flew in a few arcs around the two of them. Causing the couple to be propelled around by his gravity and inertia.

He stopped, and they did as well. *"Behold,"* he said as he directed their attention forward, the sun crowned the horizon. It looked like a ball of flame, and it was getting bigger and bigger.

The couple held each other in an embrace. For, she had broken it off with Edward this very evening. Telling him that they had moved too fast, that she had already promised herself out to another. At that point, to raise Edward's spirits, Ipso had brought them up here.

"Edward?" Ipso communicated. In response, Edward gave his master his full attention. "A new day dawns," he proclaimed to his apprentice. Suddenly, he broke eye contact and flew away at speed.

The two companions followed, so as not to get left behind, or get lost.

Ipso called it *babysitting*, when he had to watch every move, they made. Edward pondered the meaning of Ipsos' words for just a moment. Then, following close behind his companions, he went in search of his destiny.

9

The Nurse came to Meredith's cell. "Are you ready Miss Hook?"

"Ready for what?" Meredith asked distractedly.

"You don't give me that tone bitch," The Nurse screamed much more enthusiastically than ever before.

"Fuck you!" Meredith screamed in return as Bliss came around the corner.

"Hey," he yelled at Mike.

"What?" he asked as he was getting up and holding his neck. He looked completely dazed as Bliss pointed the gun at him.

"Get the fuck up," he ordered.

"What?" Mike asked again. Bliss, to assure Mike he was serious, cocked the .380 small handgun.

"Get the fuck up!" Then Bliss shot the wall.

"Boom!"

The sound was incredibly loud. Much louder than any of them expected.

It ricocheted. *"Take her in here,"* Bliss ordered and waved the gun at Meredith. Mike got the *gist* of what to do.

They entered the *'Temple of the Messenger.'* The Doctor ordered Mike to tie Meridith's wrists together and set her down on the floor and then handcuff himself to the radiator.

The lights in the room started to flicker, signaling the *Master* was sending a pulse.

"Quickly nurse." She turned and walked over to a desk and grabbed a neatly folded stack of clothes and headed back off. "Excuse me, *Nurse*?"

"*Yes* Doctor," she said impatiently.

"What are you doing?"

"What you asked."

"No, *you're not."*

"But I-."

"Change *here*."

"But_."

"DO IT HERE," he screamed.

A moment later and all was ready and began the circumambulation, signaling the *opening* had begun.

"Alma Amentia," the two companions cried as they circled the *triangle of art.*

"Alma Amentia," they cried.

The nurse, in full black ceremonial robes, went to The Messenger and handed him the dagger, its red gem literally sparkling.

He looked at Meredith.

Walking over to her slowly he raised his arms. Then, as the nurse did with Morda, Bliss would do with Meredith. Everyone was ready for the worst, wondering, *'Is he really going to kill her?'*

With all his weight, he pulled down as hard as he could.

It plunged in.

In efficient, as his speed and other variables would allow, the anathema just careened through the air and it seemed to ignite a light that was blinding. It caused all to react as if they had witnessed a lightning bolt thrown by the hand of *Jupiter* himself.

10

"Anineil," the sisters spat as they all three surrounded the Archonian.

Chanting her name, the first sister came on lightning-fast. A moment later, sprang the second sister. Then the third, all in rapid succession of each other. Trying to find a hole in her strategy, about a minute and she had caught the second sister off guard.

As she came in, knocked herself effectively to the ground and out of the game, she went sprawling on her back and into the rocks that they were close to. She cried out, *"ahug!"*

The other two sisters, seizing the opportunity, both began to pull at her robes and then at her hair. It caused her to send such a pulse, so as to knock everything over that was within several yards. Not using this ability, she was a bit rusty in its usage and she sent heavy stones cascading toward the unconscious one, more rocks smashing down onto her inanimate form.

As they began their dance, one of the sisters came in fast once again and the Angel effortlessly guided the second one snuggly into two of the giant rocks. Unfortunately, the dagger that the sister wielded had wedged her in between the two boulders.

She was held taut and could not escape, screaming bloody hell.

Next, the third came in. They crashed into each other so hard as to send more shockwaves about. Two, and four, then six, rocked the whole area. She came in sooner than anticipated and by her own inertia, she got lucky and scratched the angel's other cheek.

The most fearsome of the sisters came in. She approached and acted like she was going to punch but got her arm caught in the angel's hair. As she did so, she began to let loose a war cry. Though, as a result, in so doing, had thrown herself off balance.

"Uh," she said as she lost control.

The archangel accepted the opportunity when, *'the sister;'* just switched from foot to foot and had one hand around the back of her head and the other had a hold on her leg.

She slid her along her chest, to skin the skin right off of her face.

A bloody moment later and the Angel was standing there, humbly victorious.

This painted quite the macabre horror scene.

"Do you still blaspheme?" the Angel asked. Though the sister was clearly done. *"Do you still blaspheme against Thee?"* Her head just drooped, and blood dripped in a gush all over the ground.

It was almost silent out except for a bird in the distance and the sister of the screams. The air held the scent of honeysuckle.

Then, the sounds from the sister who was in Angel's embrace became frantic. Pulling her by the neck up to the edge of the rocks that were next to the clearing to finish the job. The two wounded sisters cried, *"NO!"*

"Have mercy," said The Sister at her feet.

"Here you are begging for my mercy, even though a few moments passed, and you would have had my head. Would you have had mercy on me?"

"Yes, sister," the two conscious ones cried. The Archonian Angel raised one eyebrow and in a moment of epiphany she questioned, *'what if her Host, was to receive this husk at her feet and she took on the guise of, 'Fury?'* As

entertaining of an idea as it seemed, she was bound by a promise that she could not break.

The sky, which only moments before was about to rain, just as quickly suddenly cleared up and the deluge was held at bay.

Then, did the birds, once again, start to sing.

Chapter XIII
The burning

1

"So, I just have to walk into it?" I asked, *'Anineil,'* the Archon.

"Yes, Artist. You and your endless questions. As if I am known in all things," the angel replied, sounding a bit irritated. The last thing I wanted to do was piss her off. When I looked upon her to try to decipher her mood, she was in statue pose once again, with a smile on her face, arms slightly behind her, head bent forward a little. Her prideful beauty would rival that of *Venus*, though she does not recognize such ideas as ego. Not as complex as humans go as far as psychological manipulations, though overall, seeming much more resolute in their celestial perfected forms.

"Anineil." I looked over and I had her attention. "What's an average day for you like?"

"Day? It's the same as yours Artist. For, we inhabit the same overall Sphere of Existence. Co inhabiting the Heliosphere with, *'The Others.'* Also, *Sol*.

"The Others?" I asked seriously.

After she told me what happened with The King, and the 'Baptism,' she gave me a lesson in hidden occult things.

"Do you interact directly with ZxTxS?" Her eyes gave a pulse of a glow as she nodded her head.

"So, am I a Demu, now?" I asked a little later.

"I suppose so Artist since we are discussing it. We would not be if you weren't. For, a 'Demu,' being one who knows."

"I get it, I get it," I said. "The regular, everyday people are called, Daywalkers?"

"Artist, you have once again answered your own question," she said.

Well, you know, you have some sharp wit about yourself there, Mam?"

"I was not aware," she said, looking down at the grass. Her hair was blowing in the wind as she surveyed the area and then began to tell me what her opinion was on what I was to do now.

Then, after a few, *'Lessons,'* she told me my options. The only reason I even agreed was her charm, that's what sold me. Not her preternatural quality or shades of any kind. Not a full-proof one hundred percent plan either. No. It was her humanness. She was young at heart and her spirit of enthusiasm was refreshing. The plan was at the least, a death wish. Though, at the very most, was what she thought wisest and I was with her. She just needs to ask and I would obey.

The *'plan,'* itself, was simple. Go back and get the disc and Talisman, take it to where it was created and let whatever elements that played a part in its creating, be the ones involved in the *unmaking*. In this case, un-forged.

To do that, we would have to go on the same trail that a man named Ipso the pure,' of Ha-Aretz traveled not so long ago.

Rumor was, that the old sorcerer had been dead for a decade or more. Well, after I was to arrive there, to the compound, I was to perform a *banishing*, and an *'Opening by East Gate Ritual,'* and that was *when* and *if*, we even make it there. Once those steps are complete, I was to make a protection circle of my own in the same *'Sphere of Existence.'* The Archonian blessed me with the correct names for invocation. Then, effectively, sealing the circle.

Assuming all this were to work, then this thing that is behind me, that's bound to me somehow, will be released and expelled to plummet back to the eternal darkness, from whence it crawled out of, or that's what I'm assuming at least.

That is, this centrifuge of perpetual existence. The Archonian spent some time with me, explaining more and revealing unto me small charms and razes which I picked up on quickly. She taught me *Rau*, that raw energy that is like, though not as powerful as, *Thaumaturgy*. That well from which is tapped that divine essence of *'will,'* to be directed by the conjurer. *'Emendatory translations,'* she called them. Being the actual name of the act of ZxTxS, an emanation, blessing the *Helioespherian* with the rare magic pulled from Himself. The *Emanations of Emanations.* The Rau Giver in him and his child, *The Osirian Manifested Self Sacrificial One* and *The Mother, ASHURA.* The female aspect of the trinity. Also, the two *Opposers*, feeding the nourishment for the gods or the *Ancients of Ancients,* it's from the radiation from the *Nechash* and *The Demiurge.*

This was all too much; I couldn't fathom all this insanity. She slowed it all down a bit. I had spent all that time searching for answers, realizing in retrospect, that the journey was the same as the sum of the experience, as with most things. In some cases, being understood way too late. Then, the wisdom to pick from the pieces, to use the experience as armor, of one strength or another. I thought, *'why don't you try to kiss her.'* Looking up, I made sure she hadn't read my expression. I smiled, entertaining the thought, that at least she cannot read minds.

Now, I just had to walk through the monolithic obelisk before me. *"Hold on.* So, I could have walked through this, *at any time?"* I asked.

"Yes," she said. Now, standing in, *'statue pose,'* of a different sort and I wanted to jest with her, though, I figured now was not a suitable time.

I took my first few steps and was within inches of Ha-Aretz and I stopped. Looking at the Angel and tried to read her expression, noticing her eyes looking in my direction, but past me, this seemed to be true to her nature.

"Artist," she said. I started to brace myself for an impending lesson of a different kind, though when none was forthcoming, I looked a bit closer and sure enough, she was in a different pose. This time I saw, she was saying goodbye. Winking at her I started walking and felt a Volt of electricity Ohr lighting me up.

The scintillations burst all around me and coercing my atoms to make up protons and matrons, crashing together and being reborn. Beholding atomic nuclei disengaging and spinning around my soul, carrying it and its mocking echo so that it bounced back, just like the Doppler effect.

The Vortex took me.

2

There I was, to be shat out on the other side of the wormhole. I had made it inside the area known as, *'The Manx.'* My echo strangely mocking itself. Then, one way riding the atoms amid Tohu Vavu just to be assimilated back into this reality's version of my physical existence.

It was then, that I saw that eternal serpent and at that moment I suddenly realized this was, *'The Nachash.'* That was its name, its symbol was an infinity knot turned on its side, *—the devouring cannibal. The consummate lovers. The sacrificial scorn* of the *Demiurge. 'To know it is to live a thousand years,'* they say.

Lightning licking here and there all over. It was like a blanket of fog that encompassed me within this Merkabah. Light began to scintillate and the outer edges expounded. Then, that sound of an adorning buzz ceased itself and caught flame just to be extinguished, though that little sign opened all the possibilities. I felt that this, *'vehicle,'* I was in, was safer than previously considered.

As the fog lifted, I stood up. For, when going through The Vortex, I had to lean down to keep hold of my balance.

Upon arrival, the smell of brimstone was strong as sparks popped here and there about the edges of the circle.

As soon as I stepped out, I looked around. Gate particles, biomechanical, closing within my Sphere of Existence. Smoke blanketed the floor, obscuring its surface momentarily. All was exactly as I had left it, even the sarcophagus. Looking over at the *'Occupant,'* yes, he was the same as was everything else that was in the chamber.

Good.

At least no animals or anything like that got in. I found my bag and retrieved the metal disk and then started to search for the Talisman the Angel had told me about.

After looking everywhere within reason, I set down to rest once again. Getting into position with being so aggravated, I had to keep reminding myself to breathe and think clearly. Closing my eyes, I did just that.

Then, with my third eye open, I started to scan over my vicinity as I focused on getting my breathing under control. I was so warm that I decided to keep my eyes closed.

Figuring, I would meditate for a bit, my head drooped, and I at once fell into unconsciousness, for I was beyond tired.

3

Upon realizing she was dead, Morda at first thought she felt worse, though overall, she was feeling the better for the wear.

For one, her mind had cleared and she could talk plain now. It had been, it seemed years since her physical body could support a conversation without some spirit or mindless mass stealing her attention away. Now that she was on this plane, she had the chance to be someone, because sadly, The Terra plane, had offered her little in life.

After she died, she met up with a few old friends. One was Edward Hook. He needed her help, she was like, *"I cannot even die and be left alone,"* then they laughed. Great friends, they were.

He told her that he was limited in who he could communicate with and he had done all he could in the form of a shade. He explained to her that after he went back to try to completely stop the intruder from all those years ago, he ended up only being able to lock Edna into the bathroom. For one fleeting glimpse, she had stared back at him through the mirror, though she was frightened.

Now, here I was with Mordas incorporeal form, in the basement with me, which was strange because she was a ghost. When she appeared, I was making sure the gun that I had found was loaded.

"Holy shit," I said as I ran my hand gently through her smoky form.

"There's not much time," She explained impatiently.

"What do you mean?" I asked. "No one even knows about this place, besides," looking over at the previous occupant

"I'm supposed to tell you, if you want to behold the brightest light imaginable, well, you better help me get the 'Lady of Suffering,' *with you.* We don't have much time, we must hurry.

"OK," I said as I just watched as she ran around the room, putting different things together into a backpack.

Another moment later and we were standing around the borders of the circle.

In this work, I was an assistant. Once everything was ready, she went through all the motions seamlessly. The ritual would work perfectly she assured me. After completing the invocation, smoke appeared like ghosts at the edges of our vision, which was everywhere in this place and will always be a fixture in Mordas, *Sphere*.

Then, something came out at the sides of the circle, splashing way up and over, until there was a loud Tesla coil-like popping , akin to a circuit breaker or gunshot. "Artist," Morda said.

"Yes."

She ran her hand over the top of the circle where the mysterious matter was wetting the edge. Scooping some of it up, she said, *"Qualia."* I understood. This was the *physical, mailable,* representation of *reality*.

Existence itself, in the form of Hawking Radiation splashing up and over in small plums. "So exceedingly rare to have a glimpse," she said as it poured through her incorporeal form.

"Shouldn't it be pulling us into a black hole, being so close an all?"

"It's *basically* a *synthesized strain.*"

"So, it's kind of *fake*?"

"*Absolutely not.* How do you think were sucked into The Vortex and then spat out the other end?"

"I don't know, splitting atoms and sending a proton in one location, and a neutron in the other?"

"Half correct. See you don't know everything. Haha, ha. I'm just messing with you, it's not that serious," she jested.

"You don't call that, serious?" I asked, pointing at the corpse.

"You're just missing the main ingredient. *Qualia*"

"Um, Morda?" I said, pointing to the *'Circle.'*

There was the hum of electricity as our hair was lifted amid a light popping sound. Followed by small orbs popping all about. Atoms smashing together, creating matter.

Within the mysterious liquid, a form began to appear as a silhouette of a skeleton and then morphed into a tenuous thing. At once a furor sprang to manifest, as there appeared *'the woman of suffering.'* She looked like she was sleeping and beautiful to behold. The more she assimilated, the more she reminded me of a mummy that has come through time, demanding its immortality.

She had dark hair with pale white skin. Her physical property's information swirled extremely fast around the circle in atomic form and then a moment later and she first started to appear. Lightning popped and the current cracked along the shores of the circle's reality. "The liquid reality, you see Qualia. Its origin, that the Patriarchs subscribe to, is Andalusian, from the Nocturnity River," Morda told me.

Then, the woman of suffering arrived.

Upon opening her eyes, she looked at me, then toward Morda. Her eyes looked glazed; she was sick, I could tell. When she got up a moment later, she went into the bathroom with Morda to clean up.

After several moments they came back out. I thought Meredith was genuinely nice. Hearing her cry, I stayed over on the couch to grant them a bit of privacy.

The woman was related to the dead man; he was her grandfather. Then, they both started looking for something. A few scattered moments later, finding it on a necklace on the old man's person, she and Morda started searching the desk. After digging through the drawers, they were stuck.

Then, asking for help, I went over and dislodged one of the drawers from underneath the desk. Inside I found a box and gave it to them.

I stepped back to just observe as they began to examine the box's contents. Morda's incorporeal frame, and I knew what to do.

Morda, after helping pull Meredith through, had filled her in on what was going on.

As they tried to think of where this Talisman was, surprisingly they found it. It wasn't too difficult, for the desk had a hidden drawer, which held a box with the talisman inside that Meredith remembered from so long ago.

Next, they just had to take this object and the disk back to whence it was created.

Morda knew all the invocations needed once we were to get there.

Now, just to get them out of here, and into one of Edward's cars.

Morda's concentration was broken when a slight tempest built up around them, and about the circle. Knowing full well what this sign meant, they quickly grabbed the sets of keys and headed out.

As they were shuffling to get everything, they needed, The Vortex, within the Circle, began opening.

Small electro-charged particle bubbled along the edges and started to pop. Silhouettes of three figures began to appear. Upon exiting the room, they ran into, then out, the sarcophagus.

Just as they were through, bright Ohr started to lick the circle edge.

4

"There's no fuckin way," Mike said aloud when Meredith vanished amid a furor of lights.

The drama had risen to quite the climax. The doctor's scream still echoed all around the stone walls. The Nurse was quickly putting out a small fire that had started on one of his sleeves. He just looked in a daze, mouthing unintelligible words.

"I lost it," the Doctor said. *"I lost the sacrifice."*

"No, we got the main one, The Master requested," reasoned The Nurse.

"*How* did that *happen*?" He asked.

"I don't know, but I have a feeling we're about to find out soon enough," she said thoughtfully. Mike walked up and put his hand on the stone. It was already getting cold. Both senior hospital staff members just watched Mike. Standing back up his knees popped.

"Mike, is it?" The Doctor asked.

"Yeah, why?" Mike asked in response.

"I thought so. I want to get your opinion on it."

"On what?"

"Oh, this thing," Bliss said reaching onto the table and grabbing a magazine. It was rolled up and he carefully untied a string that was wrapped around it.

Then, opening it, he found where the bookmark was, and pulled out the handgun that he had shot Brady with.

"Ok," Pointing it at Mike he said, "sorry."

"Boom! Boom! Boom! Boom! Boom!"

As the lights flashed in his direction, Mike thought, *'will he ever stop shooting me?"*

5

"Make sure he's dead will Ya?" Murry asked.

"Yes Doctor," she complied. When going over to Mike's body, The Nurse quickly knelt and checked his pulse, she turned, *"He's alive."*

"Great," he said making his way past the table and chair. Then, leaning over and grabbing his hands, he pulled, clearly mad. He growled. She hated when he would act like this. Appearing to be out of control is what it was. He stopped whatever it is he was doing. *"Will you help me, Nurse?"* He yelled.

"Of course," she said. Jumping into motion like she had a delayed reaction. She must have been in a daze as she self-consciously looked over. He met her gaze until she looked back down. Shaking his head back and forth as they moved the body into the Circle with a grunt, dropping it with a thump. She just stared at him.

"You know you give me the creeps sometimes," he said.

"Ah," she cried jumping away from the circle but falling because her hand on Mike wouldn't let go of her ankle. Now it was Bliss that was just staring. *"Help me,"* she called. Going over he grabbed his gun off the table.

"It's too late," she said somberly. Murry, coming over and looking down and yes, he was gone by the looks of what came out of his mouth.

Following the trail of black clotted blood across the floor up her shoe," raising his eyebrow. "And it's all over your legs," he said looking up. When he got to her face, The Nurse's look, was one of *ferocity*.

Mike, in his death, throws had vomited thick streams of yesterday's dinner all upon her righteousness. Maybe, it was one last irony thrust upon The Nurse, for her abolition of evil? Maybe, Mike was simply reflecting back what *she* projected *onto* others?

"I'll be right back," she said and trailed off but stopped dead in her tracks. The lights started to dim a bit. Going in and out of the room from the electricity.

The Circle started to glow white-hot with Mike in the center.

Then, a small arc of light jumped from the Circle to the Triangle of Art, igniting the Sphere.

"Quickly, the Trill," Murry said.

Going over to the table she grabbed a small metal box; out of that, she took another box with a little belt attached. This one she opened and popped something into then closed it. Sliding her index finger to the corner she pulled out one, then two, small rocks. The third was what she popped into the device. She walked over and handed it to him as he was sitting on the stone floor, next to Mike.

The Nurse went to just inside the first ring of the Circle and put one on each side from which the Doctor was sitting. Thus, creating a triangle of Art to Manifest. "Is that it Doctor?" The Nurse asked.

"For now," he said and then had an out-of-body experience like his, *'Other,'* took what, 'The Patriarchs of the Eternal Flame,' refer to as, *Achuzzan*. Or what we call here on Ha-Aretz; Possession took control.

A few moments later and their Master had told the two Messengers what to do to accomplish the goal of killing the woman and using the blood sacrifice of the Daemons enemy's blood relative.

Then, use all this to invoke Begrevra, the Destructionary, safely through unto physical manifestation.

To bring about as many Daywalkers' demise as possible. After the two Worshipers dragged Mike's body out of the way, they quickly stepped into the *'Circle.'* A light tempest began to spring to manifest as the electricity faded in and out of the appliances of the chamber's circuits. A moment later and they were gone, in pursuit of the escapees.

6

We made it through the corridor and outside. Once free, we realized it was still pitch blackout. "Be careful, and stay close, "I told Meredith.

"I know it's bad out, here," she said. "If you're not from around here."

"Have you met the neighbors?"

"Yeah, Lou and his kids."

"I don't know, I didn't catch a name," I said, "from there, right?" Pointing in the direction of the house with the screen door.

"That's the one," as if that were the signal the kitchen light came on. I perceived the sound of voices on the right-hand side of the Opera House of some animate shadows moving about.

"What is it?" Meredith whispered as to my reaction to impending doom.

"Quickly, to the garage," we both went in that direction, except for Morda, who went back the way they had come.

"Psss, Morda," Meredith hissed after her. She just kept going, smoke trail behind her levitating mass.

"Come on, we gotta go. She'll be fine," I said. "Do you know the fastest way into the garage without going around the front?"

"Yeah, over on the side, I have the key. I can tell it's a double of the one I have somewhere upstairs in my room." At this realization, Meredith felt a ping in her chest of longing.

It's strange but I felt her sadness, so I grabbed her hand once again to keep her in good spirits. *"Come on,"* I said. Then, turning to go we both gently bumped into the grandson and his daughter from across the alley.

"Wow, where you gone try to get off to?" The man said. Then the girl started getting excited.

"Merry?"

"Kendra?" Meredith asked but knew.

"You know me, yeah, you do me," the woman said.

"Kendra, where's your pa?" She asked.

"He coming, he went a go get shoon," she said.

"What?" I asked.

The siblings together said it again, though still, it was mostly unintelligible, the only word we understood was, *"shoon."* We both looked at each other and mouthed the words, *'shotgun.'*

In the house from which they lived, across the alley the back doors screen squealed open and there was grandpa. "Uh, wan, see?" Said the pregnant woman.

"What?" Asked Meredith. At that point, the back door to the corridor screamed open.

"No, we don't wanna see your baby, but you see that door?"

"Yeah."

"There's a guy with a woman about to come out that door," I said pointing.

"Uh?" She asked. *"Wha de want?"* She asked.

I got down a little and clandestinely told her and her brother, "they are the state workers."

"Yeah, wha de want?"

I began pointing at the woman's belly and raised an eyebrow. "*To* take, *Da* baby."

"What?" They both said startled. As if this were the most atrocious crime ever uttered. Presently, the door to the corridor was wrenched open. At the same time, the engorged one screamed."Wampa ooot em!"

"Boom!" The shotgun flashed from the old man on the back porch. Grabbing Meredith's hand I said, "come on."

"Hold on," the woman had Meredith's wrist.

"Let go," I told the woman sternly. She looked straight in my face; I could smell the rot upon her.

"Hold on," she said again. Only this time looking directly into Meredith's eyes. *"Old on, take me."*

That is when her brother's head was slightly knocked to the side. Twice. His eyes rolled a bit and in that instant, he grabbed his head yelling. The woman went wild, letting out a howl such as I have never heard.

"Come on, we must go," Mordas's translucent frame ordered us, but we didn't have to be told twice.

As we rounded the corner of the door to the garage, we could hear more gunshots amid screams of *"kill ew. Kill ew."*

Before long, making our way into the garage, once inside, Meredith took over. I gathered myself for a moment and after a second later I was ready to leave.

Looking around the inside of the car she became nostalgic and told Morda that she knew it was his vehicle, she was just never able to find the keys. Figuring she would one day, now she was glad she had never gotten rid of it.

"You *do know*, someone *has* driven this in the last few months, *right*?"

"There is no way. I park on the other side of the garage every night and I would have known."

"Ok."

"What? You don't believe me?" She asked.

"No, I do," I said smiling.

"Guys?" Morda called from the back seat. Her incorporeal forms eyes glowed yellow. "Guys?"

"Yeah, what's up?" I asked. Though, just by her expression I knew to look in the rear-view mirror.

Just then a white car appeared back in the other lane, locked in traffic about five vehicles back.

"Them fuckin bastards took me forever to save for that thing," Meredith said.

"It's ok," Morda reminded her. "You can get another one."

"Ug," she responded.

"Up here make a right," Morda directed. Behind them, the white car came up and went past without noticing them.

"Is it always so busy over here in the wee hours of the morning?" I asked. Meredith and Morda just laughed as we went through the intersection, being stopped by yet another light.

"Ok, so after this light at the gas stations, keep going straight."

"Get onto the turnpike and head, I mean, take 64 West to Imperial." I looked over and Meredith had been looking at me I knew, and I was blushing.

Good, the light turned green.

"Do you think we should grab gas, let me know?" I asked as I started to pass the stations that were on either side before jumping onto the interstate.

"Yes," Meredith said. "I mean, pull over please."

"Sure."

"Just pull in," she said.

A moment later and we were parked. She looked over at the gas gauge. "Nah, we'll be fine, we don't need any." Then, she appeared to be thinking extremely hard.

"What is it?" Morda asked from the backseat.

"I think we are going in the wrong direction. Can you, um, talk to, him?" Questioned Meredith.

"Oh, sweetie. Oh sweetie, He is not, *real*, in the sense, that you think He is"-, Morda began.

Meredith giggled, cutting the older woman off, "not Him. *Grandfather*."

Looking down in contemplation she said, "I did, for a moment. I have no idea now, this is all so new to me and there seem to be many doors, just most are locked." For the first time, I saw this Morda, wasn't the pinnacle of self-confidence she seemed, she was afraid.

She was a soul. Fundamental Pureness.

Then, a curious thing happened. Meredith, grabbing Mordas hand, let a tear escape.

The ghost, with letting a tear-out and her sharing the moment, let her fall. Though, upon spilling down her cheek, it quickly evaporated in the early morning traffic lights. The way that they can.

"Ok. So where exactly are we going?" Morda and I waited for an answer.

"I was going to have you ask my grandfather, but I know where were off to," she said dramatically looking at the shade in the backseat.

"Ok? And?"

"Not to this other man Ipsos, or whatever. We need to take it back to where this all started, with my family," she said distantly with a faraway look in her eyes.

"Cahokia," Morda, with that same look of despondency. *"Quickly, make a right out over here and let's jump on the bridge, there,"* she said pointing.

I put it in drive and pulled out, followed by two short rights and we jumped onto the bridge, on our way into Illinois.

"How long till we get there?" I asked. It seemed like they were both going to answer me at the same time when again, they were quiet.

Meredith, breaking the momentary silence said, "about thirty minutes." Then, we were all gazing at the blood-red streetlights as they started to fade as the night gave birth to inky black skies and yellow lines on the road that seemed to go on and on forever. The humid air coming through the windows was honestly refreshing. For, I hadn't even recognized I missed it so.

When Meredith realized they had to, instead of taking the Talisman to the old compound, they should take it to Cahokia Mounds from whence it came. Thereupon, they would perform the invocation at dawn, to release the curse. She wasn't completely sure that it would work. Something in her gut told her to go there instead.

Speeding, they made it there in about twenty-five minutes.

Meredith thought this had been a crazy journey; she would never take anything for granted ever again.

As soon as they got out of Edward's car they looked for which way to go. There was a small guard's shack that led around a Cul de' sac that gave unto The Heritage Museum. One thing the companions noticed was the blackness. It was so incredibly dark

"How long do we have until sunrise?" Meredith asked the Artist quietly.

"About thirty minutes give or take," he answered. Suddenly, all their attention was taken aback when they saw it.

They just stood and marveled at the huge earthen barrows that dominated the view. It resembled a ziggurat, the step pyramids predecessor of the Middle East. *'The Great Mound'* in its resemblances was not unlike those, *'Land of the Gods'* structures.

The South American pyramids. Being most likely an idea brought by the game chasing Asians who traveled across the frozen waists at the end of the *'Last Ice Age.'*

Meredith followed behind Morda and the Artist.

Maridith was glad to be with her friend again. This guy that Morda said was *'invaluable'* was also charming. Meredith was smiling as she was thinking about going home.

The Tumuli were amazing; she could see now why her grandfather thought it was so magnificent. These thoughts were broken by a loud crack, then two more. She and the Artist both sunk. Even Morda slumped down.

"Pop. Pop, pop!" The Artist had a handgun of his own he had from his bag. The sounds were loud but not as much as in the hospital.

As Meredith was thinking this, she absentmindedly looked at her hand. There was something black all over it, like black water, or oil. Had she sat in something?

At once she realized it was blood. "Oh my God." The only reason she knew for sure what it *was*, was that it was so warm and sticky.

"What's wrong, Meredith?" Morda asked, looking towards the Artist and then back to Meredith. *"Oh my God, you've been shot."*

I aimed once again because I thought I saw movement by the guard shack.

7

'Good,' the nurse thought a second after Murry shot at the company that had just arrived.

"Yep, I got her," Murry said to the nurse though, it was all with the aid of Begrevras gifts she knew.

Before long, in response to Murry's gunfire, there were three return shots in retaliation. The sounds tore a hole in the night.

The Nurse was in a daze. She would be so glad to see all this dark business over and done with. It seemed like a never-ending nightmare and thereupon, Murry could be all hers. This is what she was thinking when she tried to warn him that she saw sparks and an accompanying, *"pop, pop,pop,"* that followed.

Then, trying to speak but nothing came out of her mouth, nothing except for two small puffs of smoke. However, two sister vapors were issued from her neck holes. A couple of missed shells sent reflections from the Moon upon their collected eyes. Grass and dirt shot up into the air, getting into The Doctors mustache. He wiped it away though in his attempts it only smeared into war paint.

The Nurse collapsed. Semi dewy earth soiling her carefully pressed uniform. She seemed to burp as her neck swelled a bit in size. A moment later and with the spent breath, she was left with just two vampire gunshot wounds and blood smeared around her mouth.

It appeared as if she had dark red lipstick on.

At that point, she violently jerked once in the throes of spasm. For a moment she completely ceased moving. The only sound that could be heard was the crickets and locusts. The Doctor was reminded of his fish tanks at the hospital because there was a pool thet was forming in the nurse's front.

A moment later and her excretions had ceased, leaving a pool of piss upon her. Or it looked more like *'The lake of yellow piss and vomit,'* the Doctor thought.

Presently, the *Master* was sending a communication through the Trill Device, that was bound to Murry's head.

"Arur Ohr." Begrevra intoned, his Echo being received via *'Phylactery.'*

"Arur Ohr." The Messenger answered in the hissing tones of, 'The Naga.'

"Your cohort is dead," he hissed. Words trailed out as a forked tongue licked at the air in between intonations of the ancient speech. Sounding like he was a snake.

"Yes," the Messenger answered, coldly looking down at her body. He lightly put a boot to her cheek and gently kicked her face the other way, to not have her staring at him anymore. The two gunshot wounds in her neck looked just like two vampire bites, a drop of blood barely escaping each.

"It's unfortunate, but" he hissed, *"so is, the lot, of life."* There was a brief silence, then, *"a gift for your suffering."*

"A gift for my suffering," the Messenger mocked the Echo through the channels of the Heliosphere and The Nurse just looked up into a sky that would never be shared with her beloved Doctor Murry Bliss, ever again.

8

Mike opened his eyes. He didn't know what was going on except his neck didn't hurt anymore, which was strange because, *'holy shit,'* he thought to himself. Holding his hands out to inspect them, the same familiar tattoos were there.

'Damn.' Whatever it is he had been thinking, he lost it.

He felt, very confused.

What had he been doing?

I was just talking to someone, but who? He thought of Ernie and how he was *dead*. In a flash of recognition, it all came back to him. The murder of the cop, and *Ernie*. Then, they were going to kill that, *Lady*.

"Bamm!" She had disappeared.

Next, was *his* turn to *die*.

They shot me, he mused. Thereupon he gazed through his incorporeal hands.

There were the two pieces of shit now. Hiding on the side of the small guard shack, kissing. He felt his gorge rise.

Everything was smoky and cloudy for Mike. Phantoms danced in and out of his peripheral vision. Looking closer, he saw there were these specters all over. He instinctively knew they were put here to be the guardians over the burial grounds.

In his mind's eye, he could see teepee tents and huts, little fires going out of the chimneys. It was very dark and gloomy, even then.

Shamans began beating their magic wands upon the drums of death during a ritual. The Nurse began to give the doctor a hand job. Mike just watched until completion.

When he saw the car lights a moment later, that's when The Doctor had fired that damn gun.

The shots made everything glow for no more than a sixteenth of a second. Then, The Nurse bitch slumped over dead. She had it coming though, he thought, for his justified anger.

Now, the doctor was talking to someone that Mike could not see nor hear. He still had that strange box strapped to his head. What did he think, that he could talk to aliens through it? Mike scoffed.

Then, slowly looked up and back down at the scene unfolding around him. It was a very frightening thought.

Imagine a prominent Doctor that, during the treatment of patients had been going mad most of his professional career. Talking to himself with boxes strapped to his head and war paint on. He giggled.

Then, it was as if hundreds of people were all showing up at the same time.

Here to see what happens next?

Mike ran atop one of the smaller mounds to get a better look.

Yes, his vision was not deceiving him. Hundreds of people had just seemingly shown up. It must be because The Doctor is talking to someone on that strange Bluetooth headpiece or something, he reasoned.

Then a raccoon, or no, it was a hand, breaking dirt at Mike's feet. He fell in horror as it tried to grab at his ankle. He moved his foot. Then it tried to grab that. A skeleton's arm went around his neck and at the same time another one was wrapping its arms around Mike's waist. The embrace of ages.

"Ahhhhh," he yelled. The smoke was caught up by their movements. Ignorantly going through his incorporeal form like it could attack the smoke.

Mike jumped up and away, past the reanimated bodies that were escaping their earthen graves. One broke ground and stood. After steadying itself. It bounded for him and then passed, seeing a fresher target.

Getting to his feet, he ran the dozen or so yards to an already vacated area. Every tumulus had at least a couple hundred of its previous inhabitants all seemingly trying to get out of the Earth at the same time.

The dead were rising out of the barrows in Cahokia.

Chapter XI
Raising the Dead

1

"Bammmmmm!" The door to the museum was busted open.

"Come on," Morda yelled to the companions.

The Artist helped Meredith down so she could sit and rest very gently next to the wall.

Then Morda, going and locking the front door, noticed the blinds in the front window in the room that we were currently in, were cracked.

Gazing out into the inky blackness she thought that there might be a concert or something going on tonight that she wasn't aware of. Blinking her eyes several times, she peered back out.

Being held in a slight suspension of disbelief. What was happening out there? With this new sight, she could see auras and strange color combinations. If that's what it was that she was seeing.

All these concertgoers or whoever the people were that had just seemingly shown up by the hundreds were already dead. She could tell by the phosphorescent hues that they gave of.

Skeletons. Reanimated corpses. Morda put her hand to her mouth. "Oh no," she lightly whispered to herself. Realizing the implications of this turn of events.

"What's going on out there?" the Artist asked. At this question she was brought back to the situation at hand.

"Help me find a first aid kit," Morda said.

"OK, I'll be right back." Seeing the look of anxiety on Meredith's face, he walked over to her and pulled out the handgun from his back pocket. "You know how to use one of these?"

"I'll show her," Morda said taking the weapon.

"Ok cool." He jogged toward a door with lights on behind it. Disappearing a moment later.

"Now, let me see you," Morda ordered. Meredith started panting with anxiety.

The older woman got down on her haunches to examine the wound more closely. "Ah! It looks like it just passed right through at the middle." She smiled at Meredith; Meredith smiled back. The Artist was coming back down the hall.

The low night lights that had been on when they got inside were sufficient to see by after coming in out of the darkness of night.

"OK, so, I found this," he said. Handing her a first aid box and a bottle of water. Morda went shuffling through the kit and fished out a packet of medicine. The Artist handed her a handful of paper towels.

"Thrahshhhhhhh!" A sound like someone threw rocks at the windows startled them.

The Artist, peering out of the blinds, jumped back surprised, he said,*" holy shit!"* Then stopped, gazing at Morda. Her look checked him. It said, *'don't you dare make the situation worse.'*

"Um, what I meant was, damn, it's incredibly dark out there."

"It sure is," Morda said looking directly at him. "It's dark in here too." With the two of them acting *so strange, Meredith tried to get up.*

"What is it?" she asked, trying to stand.

"No!" Both yelled in unison.

"It's nothing," said the Artist. Morda was putting pressure against the wound as she saw the him wearing a look as if he were torn between something. Then, looking at Morda he began, "there's no way Bliss and the Nurse could have raised all of them all by themselves. They had to have had help."

"I don't know for sure, but I do know one thing, here, *anything is possible."*

"What do you think it is?"

"I think your right, he's getting help from someone," she mused.

"Right, because if he would have had this power all along by himself, he would have used it before now. I would imagine."

"Wait, what? What are you guys talking about?" Meredith asked.

Morda gently looked over into Meredith's innocent eyes and said," the dead are rising, and we gotta get that disc up to the top of Monks Mound by the light of dawn."

2

This was too much excitement for 'The Messenger' to take. He was hard right now watching the inhabitants of the surrounding barrows seeking humanity once again. All those rotten bodies that were so shallowly buried. Not very much help though. In numbers, they could do some damage. They did appear menacing, however, in reality, being just some bones. Not extraordinarily strong, The Messenger thought, Murry Blisse's other self. And poor Nurse Margaret's dead.

He wanted her to rub him off. He would kill that guy that they had with them.

Damn, why did she have to get herself shot? This complicated things. Well, that's not too bad he supposed. A lot more could have gone wrong.

One of the skeletons which still had a lot of meat and some flesh on it had a traveling companion. Although, his bottom half had a type of slimy oily flesh wrapped over his top half. However, most of the unfortunate walker was all rotted away and what was left besides was just splintered bones and a configuration of maggots and worms.

Peering through the gloom with half-turned reptilian eyes, he realized the corpses that weren't buried deep enough in the shade, time had rendered their skeletons *brittle*. The ones that were now rotten and whose innards were now crawling with life of the insects of generations past, had sported columns of evolutionary progression anywhere and everywhere it would thrive.

Now, here were two that were not nearly buried deep enough. Both had had their hearts cut out, sporting holes in the center of their chests. Though, still, they held hands. Soul mates must really be connected through the soul. For, their hearts were non-existent in their bodies. Reminding Murry of all those evil patients that claimed that their evil behavior was because they didn't have a heart. Well, he thought, as the macabre couple limped by, they were clearly confused about reality. Yet, these lovers amid dirt and time still holding on to each other under the pale moonlight. Together again, upon Ha-Aretz, for one last dance.

3

Mike did not like this at all. Even though he was dead, he found a spot out of the reanimates way. There were so many of them. A few thousand or more and that was not even exaggerating.

Moving in big waves. He was trying to notice a pattern. The mounds were not the only place the creatures were coming from, even the flatlands held huge chunks of them.

Mike didn't know if he had ever seen as many people as this, let alone dead ones. He was starting to be able to tell what things were from farther away by the colors they produced. Then, casting a wary glance around, he realized the Moon and the Sun, were interacting with all animate matter about him. They were casting an Aura on the undead people now.

Alive people. Dead people. Good and Bad. They all had their hue, and in turn, one could see another's biological makeup of a being. As these thoughts moved about his mind, some he knew, some he just didn't understand, but mostly he didn't care unless it was affecting him and these damn dead bodies, they were affecting him, he longed for his life he had.

"Hey." Mike was a little startled when he heard the voice. He was expecting The Doctor to be on Bluetooth or something, but it wasn't. It was a lady. It was someone, *familiar*.

Peering through this gloomy new world he found himself a part of, he quickly realized it was the lady *Morda, from the hospital.*

"Huh?" He questioned the semi-transparent form that was now before him. He was surprised that she not only could see him, but she was talking to him. *"Morda?"*

"Mike? *It's you,*" she said, happy to see a familiar face. *"I'm so glad that we've found you,"* she spoke in that soft voice that was now *bold* and *strong*. Though, still being warm and somewhat motherly at the same time.

"We've?" He asked.

"Oh, um. Do you remember a recent patient? She was in the day room last night with me when you came and got me for Meds?"

"Yeah, for sure. Um, but she's gone now, right?" At this misunderstanding, Morda looked confused.

"Really?"

"Yep."

"What do you mean?" She asked again, clearly confused.

"Well, Um. It's like you would have to of been there to believe it," he reasoned. Not really having the words to explain what had happened when she had disappeared into the doctors' hidden chamber.

"No, I get it," she said. Upon her death, she had a new awareness of events. Even though she wasn't there, she only half understood her newfound capabilities. However, more insistent than all the other pressing matters currently surmounting the night, she began to take a particular interest in him. "Walk with me?" She asked as she proffered her forearm.

'Why not,' Mike reasoned to himself, not knowing that she could reasonably sense his thoughts. When he put his arm lightheartedly through hers, he now noticed how this woman was much different than the melancholy patient at the hospital. This lady was awesome. Looking over at her, he noticed how she was gazing at him, with youthful enthusiasm on her face.

"I need your help with something. A lot has changed in the last couple of hours," she said.

4

Meredith and the Artist were alone.

"Hey," she said, breaking the monotony going on outside the museum.

"Hey there Miss," I awkwardly answered, trying to sound as in control of the situation as possible. I was so shy since I had been in her presence, with her being so beautiful and all. She held this esteem in a most baroque and rococo way. She started to say something, but held back, resigned.

"No, what's up?" I asked, trying to exude as much confidence as I could muster.

"So, how do you get your eyes to glow like that? I didn't even know they made contacts that could do that." I had forgotten until now, the illumination that the Archonian had bestowed upon me.

"That is actually a funny story," however, I stopped mid-sentence, not really knowing where to begin.

"What?" She asked. "I can tell, *you* were just about to say something." At once, we both just smiled at each other. Morda had been gone for about two minutes and it was silent besides the cacophony coming from beyond the door.

"Well, um, a special friend of mine, gave them to me, as a gift." with that they instinctively glowed at a short pulse, lighting the room up momentarily.

"A girl?"

"Um, yeah, but we're just, um, traveling companions. Yeah, she's a good friend. A teacher of mine of sorts."

"Ah. Could I ask you something else?"

"Yeah, sure. What's up?"

"Would you come and sit with me?" she asked in that sweet angelic voice of her own. I then noticed her lips and eyes more fully. Her dark hair, yeah, she was something else for sure. Almost like a modern-day *May West*. I could see myself falling for such a girl.

"Of course," I said, shuffling around the room to get to her. A moment later and I was scooting down to sit beside her. We both looked down at the same time. She smiled, so I did as well. This was one of those moments to make my move.

As I closed my eyes, I really should kiss her I told myself. If any woman had ever sent a guy a sign of when to make a move, this was it. I had a green light to go. I, in most cases, just went for it. Though now, felt it would be super uncomfortable to be rejected in this seemingly untimely situation. Also, I had only just met her no more than a couple of hours hence and rather than risk ruining the moment, I held my storm in check. The last thing I wanted was for her to perceive me to be a creep or something of that nature.

I went to open my eyes and saw hers closing. Thereupon I ever so slightly felt her plush lips on mine. It was like the top was being pulled off my chest and my beating heart was warming my whole constitution.

"Boom!"

Something had broken a window. *"No, no, no!"* she said. The clamor coming from the restroom's window was left open. A decayed arm was halfway inside and as a result. A vase full of roses was knocked over causing it to crash.

'Why would anyone put these here?' I mused to myself.

One of the dead animates bony fingers were scratching on the surface of the glass. This hand was attached to a skinny wrist, that had on a big gold bracelet. It began beating a rapture of insistence upon the window. *"Tick. Tick. Tick."* A moment later, the thing wandered away.

I was back to her in no time. She put her head on my shoulder when I sat down next to her. "I'm so tired," she said sluggishly. It was so cold in here; it was hard to think and relax for a moment. Though, for some reason, none of it mattered because her hand felt so good in mine.

"I'll keep an eye on you," I said softly to her. Silently, I felt her smile by her gently squeezing my hand holding onto me.

5

Begrevra sat at the picnic table that was in his backyard. Lately, in *'Havlla Monarchia,'* it was all the rage to have a brightly painted picnic table.

-But damn, he hated it here. He had honestly only really been getting used to being a free man recently once again.

The story was, that one night after returning from Ha-Aretz on business, making the botched deal with Edward, at first, Begrevra, had the satisfaction of coming back a winner. Which means he had made his father happy, *momentarily*.

However, a few weeks later, when the deal was no longer echoing, everything went sour. Begrevra had to go to court for that unspeakable crime and was sentenced to serve at least a Till at the Work Camp Mills in The Andalusian Waists.

Needless to say, it was hard on him. He came back and was changed physically and mentally. Then, after getting out and doing minor territorial work for the 'Order of the Risen Slain,' he stumbled across, 'The Cult of the Messenger.'

Begrevra would spend hours messing with the guy, in fact, at the work camps *'That,'* was all the rage.

It was all fun and games Begrevra thought until someone takes it all seriously and has more followers than the next Demu and they perform the proper sacrifice and bring that mother fucker through The Manx. Luckily, it took so much preparation because imagine that, never seeing a Demon and all of a sudden, one appears, bloody before Thee, in all its splendor.

This Messenger, was already convinced that *he*, *Begrevra*, was a first-class Demonic God, who could do about anything.

Now, it was all over. His wife hated the 'Order.' She, being a strict Southern Baptist from Ha-Aretz didn't put up with any blasphemy.

"Give it to me," she said. He handed it over. *"No more,"* and she broke the 'Trill Phylactery Device,' into unfavorable pieces. Then, she ground them into unfixable detritus. Begrevra wouldn't be able to tap into the echo of the Heliosphere for several years to come.

Though later, he was properly converted.

6

"You ready?" Morda asked Mike.

"Yeah," he answered as he lit the lighter. The trail of gas running to the first car caught fire as a few of the bodies were ignited. Like human torches, engulfing all like a coiling snake. The reanimates just watched in confusion.

Morda, looking over caught Mike staring at her, although his attention was stolen away. She wondered who he was. Who he *really*, was inside. He had been so kind to her at the hospital, at her worst. She's had heard on more than one occasion, that if you could handle someone at their worst, then you could handle them at their best. It wouldn't be difficult at all for Morda. It was welcomed here, now.

A moment later and the car buckled and exploded.

"Boom!"

7

The messenger was exhilarated. Here came another gift from The Master.

The Daemon Andres came out of The Vortex. Smoke and small volts popped on the dewy Earth, sending up little vapors of smoke.

This Merkabah was a little different, it had bloody matter all around its points and sides. The panes were barely visible, spines being clotted with filth. It almost appeared as if the interdimensional being within had driven through a crowd of Daywalkers. However, that not being the case, because a Merkabah is not driven or ridden, they are experienced.

Now Andres, walking up to the Messenger and looking in his eyes, showed him another world entirely. Andres could have stood here and messed with these poor humans' minds for longer but then remembered that time is not only relative but foreign as well to the observer. Reading Bliss's thoughts, they started to communicate. After a moment, he was away. Heading straight for the museum.

He knew what to do.

Finally, The Messenger felt like somebody. Really somebody. However, an explosion rocked the whole area, upsetting everything.

"Smack!" Something hit him. *"Fuck!"* He yelled. There was a big piece of plastic burning the dead nurse's tennis shoe. Not an inferno or anything, just enough for her to catch flame.

"What the" Bliss said not believing his eyes. The Nurse was moving. Trying to put out the blaze, only she had that slowed down nature as with, *'holy shit,'* he wondered. She is a reanimate now.

The Nurses eyes were glowing within, though they held a blank infinite quality as well.

Bliss looked directly into them, nothing. Well, she was in better shape than everyone else here.

"What the?"

Was she? She was trying to speak. *"What are you trying to say?"* He yelled into her face. Then, he started maniacally laughing.

Gazing around, he noticed that the explosion had sent similar pieces of debris all over the area. Thus, small infernos had come to tempest all about the mile square. "Come on," he told them, The Nurse followed. "And you, hey," he yelled at the corpse of Mike that had been one of the first gifts of enchantment that their Unholy Lord Begrevra had blessed them with.

Upon his demise, he, Mike, had been connected to them, though, in turn, his soul was released. Not bound to the murderers like this physical body that *was* his.

The Messengers were to take the candidate, in this case being Mike, to the top of the mound to be possessed by the Unholy one. To bring about the dark fruit that Father VenzVoss had planted into fertile soil so long ago.

They started to make their way up the steps to the top of the borrowed hill. In the distant past, others were possessed by evil spirits who thirsted for their living blood.

8

When I saw him there in a dazed and mad fury, I watched him go all the way up the steps. So when he sent his Nurse off with that other man, I came up over the bend. Studying the scene, I tried to put the pieces together.

The Daemon was brought here by Bliss. They're only mimicking the echo that was based on the Trill device. Which are mineral rocks from another *continent*, or *world*, or other *Dimension* of existence that allows one to teleport from one device's location to another.

Damn, what was taking her so long? Then, a flicker, and another. She seemed to not be able to get the lighter to work. I specifically remember asking if she needed one and she said no. I wondered where she kept it on her where it could go through walls with her and still be lit for illuminating things?

"Holy shit," I whispered. They were splitting up. The Nurse and the orderly from the hospital. They both walked as if being drunk, on spirits. I wondered why The Doctor would allow his minions to drink on such a night. The man disappeared into the museum and The Nurse went inside the guard shack as Bliss mounted the top of 'Monks Mound,' surrounded by a chaos of infernal reanimates.

So, in theory, if one were to die, when a specific Sphere of Existence is manipulated there, that one would return. Well, if there was ever an incentive to fight, this was it. Then, I was filled with a burst of adrenaline. I started to jog through a big hive of the undead, careful to keep down.

Suddenly remembering that a few years ago I had been here with one of my friends, and upon leaving, instead of going back the way we had come, we returned down the western side of the main Mound.

Making my way up the steep side of the enormous mound and a few nervous moments later, I saw there was a trio of burning bodies. Stacked one on top of the other. In front. There he was in all of his mad glory. A strange black outfit, with blood-red symbols on it and a- box of some kind on his head. Though, what most caught my attention was the very real gun strapped to his side. At this angle, I could have sworn it wasn't in its case. With a volt of energy, I just wanted to kick his ass. I wouldn't pass up any more opportunities to take a chance at something that could change everything.

This would end now.

I came over the side of the mound and I ran up to him.

After giving him a chance by calling him a cunt, I swung. The white car of Meredith's exploded just as I hit him and to my surprise, it connected.

"Smack!"

"Boom!" This time the explosion was twice as loud. The shockwave easily pushed us both over. I tried to hit him as hard as I could because I did not want to have to even deal with this any longer. I half wished that I had not left the gun with Meredith now.

Then, he lunged and it startled me and before I got a chance to react, he was on me again, trying to wrestle me to the ground. At the odd angle, he kept hitting me albeit nothing was connecting.

With the corner of his fist, he hit the mark and it was hard enough for me to see stars but it had thrown him off his balance. I rushed into him and he fell over.

The gun fell out of his waistband, bouncing on the ground. He came up fast and tried to tackle me. Then, one of the animates tried to hit me as well. He grabbed me by my hair and tried to force me to the ground. Whenever I could get the room, I started uppercutting him and simultaneously tried to elbow him. He tried to get me into a chokehold. I grabbed his tie and yanked! Nothing. Yank. Nothing.

Then, my elbow was on fire. I knew more reanimates were still coming.

Next, a few more undead were cresting the hill. A handful of them watched, mostly the ones up here were maggot-eating corpses that were half decomposed. The biggest one I had thus far seen fell on us, mindlessly.

The Doctor mumbled a few words and several of the undead creatures held me tight. The more I tried to struggle, the tighter was their grip. Effectively, keeping me bound as the madman started to malevolently laugh.

9

Meredith could see the ever so slight start of saturation of hues coming in upon the horizon to paint the dawning sky. She ran out of the back door, alone.

It was so dark out here that at first, she was confident. However, now, amid the shadows, she was frightened.

She hit the trees.

Next, seeing the road was free of the walking dead bodies she crossed and headed straight for, 'Monks Mound.'

That old sage The Morning Star, promising all that fire is to come and you can either let it illuminate or consume you as it burns above. The choice is yours. Evening or morning.

All those bodies reminded her of fingers. There were so many of them now that it was almost unbelievable. She ran to the clearing and saw that her destination was off to the right, she almost tripped.

"-. -. -."

'What the fuck was that?' Meredith thought. That is when a very real human arm came around her neck. Then, to her surprise, she damn near effortlessly flipped The Nurse over.

She landed on her back and Meredith landed hard on her side with the effort.

"-,-,-."

'Goddamn' she thought. That wordless curse that the fucking Nurse seemed to be swearing was awful. Her leg had broken back upon itself and the bone was splintering out of her knee. Blood, the color of liquid mud drizzled all around her body. Flailing her arms, she looked like a windmill. The same black blood now coming out as vomit spewing forth from her mouth and other holes. Meredith knew she would never forget that sound for the rest of her life. Suddenly recalling, how shity that bitch had treated her. There was conveniently a stone right there. She was going to help her by bashing her fuckin brains in!

She grabbed it and pulled, *"Oh,"* she exhaled. Stopping from the sharp pain.

Then, she tried to put all this into perspective. What was their endgame? To bring about death and destruction she supposed. Seemed like a terrible way to live one's life. After all this she would never take anything for granted again.

"-,-,-."

'Fuck it,' Meredith thought, leaning up against a withered tree. It looked like a giant accusing finger. Pointing up in the sky, saying, *"Hey you, you fuck. Look what you have done."*

Though, at this point she wasn't trying to blame it on anyone. There seemed to be so many webs and layers of lies that to search for the truth is like looking to the liar for a future of honesty and love built upon sin. They could call it, *'The court of the Sacrificial Lamb,'* or, *'The entourage of the wondering Snake.'*

Then, she saw him. It was Mike the orderly lurching toward her. She got up and moved out of his way, when she did, he crashed into the tree. With a twist and a sharp pain, she landed hard, and he had managed to secure himself in its coiling finger bone. *'Holy shit,'* he was choking. She went to the backside of him and pulled on his collar and in so doing broke a gold necklace that had a crucifix attached. Both went flying and fate chose where the pieces fell.

Next, he convulsed into a fresh fit of spasms and dislodged his neck so that he was not choking.

Looking at his face closely, she realized he was *undead* as was The Nurse. Like these bodies walking around.

Then, he let out a terrible squeal and would not stop. His creepy wanting eyes were all bulged out.

10

"She's gone," Mike, changing preternatural form said as he came out of the security room at the Heritage Museum at Cahokia Mounds state historic site.

He was trying to put it all into perspective, Morda had been schooling him, or making a Demu of him since they met up. The Daemon was brought here by Bliss, they saw that personally. They are only mimicking an Echo that was based on, The Trill. A *G.P.S.,* type device.

"She's gone to the mound bless her soul," Morda told Mike.

"So, what now?" Mike asked.

Morda looked at him and smiled, "now we seem to be backed in a corner."

"You know Morda, the funny thing about corners is, until your backed into one, you never quite know what you will do until you get there?"

"Right?" She said raising one pointy insubstantial eyebrow.

"Jiggle!" Someone was trying the side entrance door to the museum.

"Quickly," she said. Then, as the side doors lock was almost immediately broken open, the front door was open wide.

11

The Demonic greaser was humming his hum. He stopped just for a moment to light a smoke. *"Pfff,"* he blew the vapor way out. It was his thing, to light one before the killing would begin. His vision got blurry and he shook his head awake. All that time in the work camps in the Andalusian mines had left its wear and tear on the old man. His scarred boots walked over littered bone and soil, squishing and cracking.

Andres told Begrevra that this was the last one. His last Murder on Ha-Aretz. Looking back just to gain an edge before he raged. An inferno it looked like, gazing into the window he could see their forms moving around.

Also, fear. He could taist it in the air, and with that thought, he let his true nature be released. A long purple forked tongue instead of flipping back and forth, just hung there from his mouth. As he walked up to the door and tried the handle, *it* felt along the bottom of the threshold, *slithering*, but just barely so.

Pulling out his butterfly knife, in one quick motion broke the lock.

The humans that were around before could sense that she was in there. He turned the handle and walked in. Taking a big drag off his cigarette he looked around and exhaled.

They had just run out the front door, leaving it wide open.

She was here, he knew it. In times of tension, Andres likes to hum. He started to do so. Where was she? He knew that old Witch. The one that must pay for Edward's part of the deal, and when Oph Hamesh, Begrevras father had called it, *'The Great Plot.'*

Now it was time to pay the piper. Walking all the way through, now he had the feeling that they were gone. What was happening? He would have to see the Doctor and ask him for some advice when this was all over with. Father VenzVoss would be expecting him before long.

"Damn," he said aloud.

As he exited, he directed a couple of the ghouls out of the way. Then, turning around he went back inside.

Next, as quietly as a killer, shutting it behind himself he found her.

There, behind the counter, with her head slumped, passed out. He stalked her into the big foyer area. Coming around the corner, Mike tackled him. The Daemon punched him in the face two times. Mike lifted him off his feet, the intruder unaware of how a ghost could attack him went to pull out his knife and instead pulled his zippo out by accident. Misjudging his balance, he was slammed.

Andres tried to grab Mike's arm but couldn't quite get a grip on his insubstantial form. Had the Demu a Trill Device, he could have, *'Departed.'*

The ghost was slippery. Mike was covered with mud and now he had rubbed it sufficiently into the Demons' face.

"FUCK," Andres yelled. Swinging wildly. He got on his knees to get up. Dazed and angry, Mike grabbed his head by the hair and slammed it as hard as he could against the tile.

He resisted, though Mike knocked him a good one and thereupon, knocked him an even better one. Then, again, ridiculously hard. Again, hard. Again, extremely hard. *Hard. Hard. Crack. Broken. Soft. Soft. Wet.*

"Mike, stop," Morda was begging him. *"Mike stop,"* she let another moment go by. *"MIKE STOP!"* she screamed. Presently jumping in his arms. He just let her hold him as he sobbed.

Sobbed for it all, Ernie, Morda. The Demons and the Angels. Soon all that could be heard were distant cries of melancholy and sadness.

Blood and brains were everywhere, practically covering every surface visible. If he were a Murder Artist, this room would be called, *'The Unbound.'*

12

Meredith was running past the three-score or more ghouls like a football player.

Well, the quarterbacks part anyway. When she ran past them, she would squeal in a girly way.

Holy shit! The sky was turning bright. There was not much time. She just had to get up to the top. The creatures had found The Nurse and The Orderly. Meredith wondered how these skeletons could make him yell like that. She wondered if The Nurse was trying to scream too.

Something must have happened because the dead bodies were attacking each other as others went into a frenzy and their bones were just splintering until they were dust. The night would give vent to the dawn shortly.

13

I slumped over. Bliss stood above like he was a demigod himself.

"Boom!" He hit me again. I saw stars and dirt. Then the bastard kicked me twice as he dodged one of the animates that had wandered toward him. Somehow, he could control them, for when I tried to get up, I was held taught still.

"Ugg," my bonds only strengthened against me the more I struggled to free myself as another reanimate was thwarted by The Doctor.

Next, taking off his gun belt, he started to circle the top of the mound.

"You know it's guys like you," he took a breath. "Always causing problems, for people." Next, he pointed at himself as he pulled a dagger out from behind his back waistband. "Like me, "he said. Then, pulling something else out as well, without looking away, "Do you know I've killed."

"Oh yeah? Do you think that makes you tough? To me, you're just the prime example of what a loser piece of shit looks like. *You fuckin coward fuck!"*

"Snap!" One of the bones that kept me bound broke in half. The Doctor looked over to where the sound came from, feigning an impressed look on his war-painted face.

Suddenly, he gave me a malevolent look as he let loose a scream and at once began his advance. Pulling at those that kept me bound, I braced myself for the end.

Then.

The film began to bubble.

Click. Click. Click.

"Boom!"

It was a gunshot…

"This is for Morda you piece of shit," Meredith screamed as she shot eight bullets from Bliss's gun retrieved from up here, scattered amid the dead, on The Monks Mound.

"Boom! Boom! Boom! Boom! Boom! Boom! Boom! Boom!" A moment later as I stood up, she eagerly handed the hand cannon over as The Doctor fell over on his side.

Getting up and approaching him, I saw his eyes were still open, though lifeless.

The two glassy things were brown without his glasses on and so strange. Two sets. Another set of pupils were bound within each iris. Two sets of retinae...

One set of humans. The other set was reptilian. "He was changing," I said.

"Into what?"

"A Daemon, by Dual Transmutation."

"A Demon with what?"

"I don't know honestly. *Something, Other."*

"You're making that shit up," she said smiling. Now, as they gazed upon Bliss a bit closer, they noticed that she had only gotten one shot off that hit him. It was in the same spot that Meredith's was. Coincidentally, as was Morda's.

Then, I fired the last round into his head to make sure he was dead.

"Boom!"

Holding Meredith at arm's length I said," Thank you."

She began to cry, instead of talking, she kissed me.

Presently, Mike and Morda came walking up. Morda still looked ever in control of herself. *"Holy shit, Mike, what happened to you?"*

"Nothing much," he said, winking at Morda. Meredith and I caught that moment between them. She laughed and then looked as if she were in pain from the effort.

The birds were beginning to pick up their morning song and so came the end of the locust dream of an eternal night. A pair of reanimated corpses came crashing through everyone. Surprising Meredith, Mike, and Morda and they all just fell.

"Damn," Mike said as both fell over each other like two drunk comrades.

All at once, all of the bodies ceased to function at the same time except for a dozen or so spread throughout the square mile they now adorned. Like a stop motion film, the characters just slumped over into a quiet and restful eternity.

When they dropped, it sounded like a bridge collapsing though. Dust in limbs. Limbs to dust. The ones still not changed back into their dead corporeal forms, went into a frenzy.

Begrevra's wife, having destroyed the resonance frequency for, The Device about twelve minutes ago. The transmission was just delayed. When the enchantments were all shades and shadows the bridge, if severed, was lost.

Now, permanently broken. The bridge from which the negatively charged Rau and Thaumaturgy shook with one last good convulsion this side of the Heliosphere.

The line of conductivity ceased and fell limp, like a broken manikin.

"Come on, let's go. Do you still have, The Disk?"

"Yes," Meredith offered it. "Here, you take it."

I just stood there, *"come on."*

"Just go," she said stubbornly.

"No. We either do this together or not at all."

"Come on, he's right," said Mike. *"Come on,"* he said again as he grabbed her hands and pulled her along.

She smiled, as they all hustled to the top of 'Monk's Mound.'

14

Morda remembered all those years ago. The three of them, *Edward, Ipso*, and *herself.*

"Behold, a new day," he had said. Then, he flew away, the same way they had come. Morda smiled. If there was one memory that she could keep ever anon, this would be it.

15

Almost five minutes later, the two couples crested the top of the steps. Right as they came up the Artist rushed with the Talisman to the summit. The Anathema itself had a red stone in the center glowing bright red, and up went the pentacle that Ipso had created those many years ago.

All this, at the same time as the Sun was crowning the horizon and the Risen Osiris was reborn to another day facing the East.

Then, I put the plan I had been forming into action. I sat the pentacle down and stabbed it with the Anathema.

It caused a sonic implosion.

I had to look away. It was painfully brighter than any illumination I had thus far beheld. *"It was as if one thousand Suns all shined at once. All at the same time,"* I said. Suddenly, it was like everything became aware of itself and had been caught up in its musings on creation but was self-conscious now.

A clockwork of parts, held in perpetual stop motion.

The wheel in the sky clicked into position as the mighty Heliosphere was laboring. Helios himself was up early, driving that chariot and giving adoration to *Lucifer*.

Yes, Lucifer was the fire that Prometheus had so valiantly shared with the world.

Prometheus.

Prometheus and Lucifer.

The Morning Star tempts all the Daywalkers with knowledge.

Gazing upon the fire of the Spheres of Illumination.

Tick.Tock.Tick.Tock.

I beheld The Nachash coiling upon itself, souls parting into emanations, then reunited to gaze in reflection.

At that moment I knew this beast wasn't my enemy.

The souls that were surrounding this, 'Sphere of Existence,' over the last few hours, were throwing its perpetual scimitars.

Like a rock into the spokes of a tire, it seemed, a small bump in the road. It did not slow down, for it cannot hear. It buckled and picked up speed.

Anineil was yelling at me, since it was with my third eye, I could barely hear it though, I knew if I listened close enough that it was there. Humming along.

At once, she stopped letting it Echo fully, and when it came off the wall of existence, returning like melancholy to me.

"Go back," the Archon told me. Turning back around, it was like all were staring at the stop motion theatre. *"Their blank stares were like someone who had looked into the sun for too long,"* Morda finished. I just stared at her. We all just stared at her.

"It was from a painting, well, actually a picture frame, with a piece of paper with that quote on it. I gave it to Ed. From before, long ago, from when we first met," she said. Looked at Mike adoringly. They all shook their head except for him; he wasn't in the Magister twos chamber to know what in the Hell we were talking about.

"I'll tell you later," Morda told him. Then, looking in the distance, one could see the glowing Arch light like a gateway to some other Hell. The Sun rose complete, fully crowned upon the horizon.

"Meredith, isn't it amazing?"

"Meredith a new dawn. *Meredith?"* And just like that by her not responding, I turned around. Her eyes were closed and I looked to Morda who was supporting her for some answer. I desperately searched her for signs of life. Left without options I looked into Mordas's warm and accepting eyes to tell me I was wrong and that Meredith wasn't dead albeit, there was no such consolation to come.

Then, going to Mike, tears were by now pouring out of my eyes and he just looked away, averting his gaze. I couldn't blame him; I might have done the same had the roles been reversed.

Morda started circling the top of the mound. My eyes started to throb and I was so hot up here. I took my shirt off and leaned down to try to get some air.

I just held Meredith in my embrace. Mike started the circumambulation and Morda again performed the *'Closing,'* and sealed it shut a few moments later.

"Hey, you," I yelled as loud as I could this time and was going to give *'ZxTxS,'* a piece of my mind.

Although it wasn't my voice that came back, it was Meredith's, saying *"Thank You,"* in reflection of the Echo and then, *"Goodbye."*

16

"And don't come back!"

"Yeah. Yeah. Yeah," I told him.

"Not cool man, I hope you feel terrible," James said. Shaking his head. Claudia Rose gazed at me from just

beyond the door, giving me the evil eye until her husband closed it.

So, I just got up and walked away. At that point my hands were tied, I couldn't make someone, *'listen.'*

It was an especially sad trip, for I had, in good conscious, gone to Meredith's mother and stepfather's home to tell them their dead daughter wanted me to let them know she was sorry for anything she had ever done and that she needed them for something. Well, needless to say, they not only didn't believe me, but they also kicked me out and told me to never come back. Well, their loss. Some souls are not meant to evolve, I guess.

In the shadow of a black path was I on; it's not so bad though, I embraced it and persevered.

When Gazing upon that Archonian Angel, her illumination awakened within me a sight that lit my way from that night at the mounds. I haven't been back since, but I do have plans to go soon.

Later, returning home, I took off my shoes and made sure the doors were securely locked. I still can barely comprehend it, the *inheritor* of the *Opera House.*

I walked into my painting studio and grabbed my writing implements and as I entered the room, I could hear my footfalls echo back to me from beyond the hall.

Thud. Thud. Thud.

I looked for my robe everywhere, the one that resembles a cloak. Just when I was going to give up the hunt and then wouldn't you know, I found it. Being stashed behind the couch at an odd angle. Before getting up, I grabbed the instrument case out from under it.

Next, I set *it* in the middle of the couch and unlatched all three hasps. Cracking the lid, I lifted it till it clicked.

I took out the instrument with its companion piece. I checked the tightness and it was ever so slightly loose.

Exactly right.

I began to play, launching into the first notes of *L'estro Armonico*. Playing it now strangely gave me the very same feeling from when I was riding The Vortex. However, it was over before it had even really begun or I had a chance to warm up.

'So is the lot, of life,' I mused.

Tick. Tock.Tick.Tock.

It was extremely quiet.

I contemplated the fact that the composition was written for two violins. I broke the silence with the first notes of a different score.

Antonio Vivaldi's, baroque classic 'Winter,' first act.

Closing my eyes to feel the strings, just to open them a moment later, she still wasn't there.

So, I looked away, feeling a pang in my chest. That old bastard, the *Helio Spherion.* ZxTxS that comes to claim his chosen. Chosen for what though? Solitary ambiguities? Dark reflections of mortality that hide behind a cold stained mirror? To muse upon in retrospect.

Well, I supposed that if something is to be gained, even if it's more of an aesthetic principle...

So, it comes in vivid glimpses in the form of splendorous epiphanies of the sort that is usually understood in small realizations in the realm of tomorrow. The seeds that are sown today bear an ever resemblance to those consequences that are rent for what's to come.

I started to imagine that out in the seats, listening or watching, she would be there.

Invoking her presence with everything that was buried within, clawing from without my undying soul breathing her into existence.

She would be there, *through the fog of vast particles of photons that remember;* it remembers only the most subtle illuminations. Thus, enabling her psychological impression to become manifest amid my current *'Sphere of Existence.'*

Her dark hair and figure sent a bolt of adrenaline into my heart, it seemed.

A light tempest spent itself into animation, kicking up a small furor of atoms that began to coalesce.

Crashing together, forming matter.

When I had finished the final note, I knew she would be veiled in shadow, out in the seats of the old Opera House.

Then slowly, she started clapping as I turned around…

Obscure Reflections at Dawn

Jack Clubb

Jack Clubb Is from Granite City Illinois, a small town in MId-America.
He draws inspiration directly from life. Outside, the sounds of industrial trains can be heard and church bells ring from several locations simultaneously. Voices travel from one of the dozens of bars from the surrounding area. The view is dominated by the massive Steel Mill Plant on one side, the churches and corner bars on the other. A local psych ward is always dumping its patients on the streets, causing madness to spread. All these elements combined, paint the canvas of inspiration for his world.
Jack is also a tattoo and oil painting artist.

Printed in the USA
CPSIA information can be obtained
at www.ICGtesting.com
LVHW011529191223
766867LV00004B/214

9 798887 574240